NOV - - 2024

HAPPY TOWN

Also by Greg van Eekhout

Voyage of the Dogs

Cog

Weird Kid

Fenris & Mott

The Ghost Job

HAPPY TOWN

GREG VAN EEKHOUT

HARPER
An Imprint of HarperCollinsPublishers

Library of Congress Control Number: 2023948451

ISBN 978-0-06-325336-0

Typography by Chris Kwon

24 25 26 27 28 LBC 5 4 3 2 1

First Edition

To my dear noisy friends, Kirsten and Aaron.

ONE

"Welcome to Happy Town. We Make Happy."

The cow-sized blimp sails over our new house, displaying the Happy Town motto in glowing letters. I still don't know much about Happy Town, but I *do* know that Happy Town doesn't make happy. Happy Town doesn't make anything. They sell everything, though: diapers, donuts, drones, phones, toilet paper, toothbrushes, lawn mowers, luggage, abacuses, applesauce, athlete's foot powder, art supplies, and thousands of other products. Happy Town is the biggest online shop in the world, and it's also my new home.

"How are you liking Happy Town?" a woman with a camera and a microphone asks Mom. When people move to

Happy Town they get interviewed for publicity and marketing purposes. It's been happening all day up and down the street.

"Everything's even better than we expected," says Mom with great enthusiasm. "It's so clean! So modern! It's like living in the future! And we love our new house . . . I mean, box."

The houses in Happy Town are all called boxes. The name fits, because all the homes are two-story boxes with sharp angles, painted the same white, gray, and pale green as the Happy Town smiley-face logo.

Stepdad Carl backs Mom up with a huge grin and a thumbs-up. "Great box. Terrific box."

The camera woman makes a "keep-going" gesture with her hand, and Mom complies: "My husband and I got our job offers two weeks ago, and we've only been in town one night, but it's already starting to feel like home. It's been the easiest move we've ever done."

Stepdad Carl backs her up with an even huger grin and a double thumbs-up.

Mom and Carl got married three years ago, and since then we've moved a lot because they got laid off from their jobs or were looking for cheaper places to live or places with better schools. I've gotten pretty good at starting over. And they're not lying; the moving process this time really was easy. We packed most of our things in boxes and put those boxes in a bigger box that got shipped to our new box. Then we walked onto a plane in San Diego and flew to Las Vegas, where we were greeted by a Happy Town guide who showed us to a driverless vehicle that took us hundreds of miles down a private Happy Town road into the Nevada desert. It dropped us right in front of our box where our stuff was waiting, and that was it.

The camera woman turns her lens on me. "And how about you, Keegan? Tomorrow's the first day of school. What are you most looking forward to?"

I'm taken by surprise that she knows my name, but I suppose it makes sense they'd know who was moving in.

"I'm looking forward to art class. The art supplies are supposed to be really high-tech and cool."

She nods approvingly.

My last school didn't even have art classes, and I'm genuinely hopeful about what Happy Academy has to offer, even if I already miss Topher and Nolan and Trin, the best friends I'll ever have. I hope they don't forget me.

"One last question for you all," the camera woman says.

"What would you like to say about Arlo Corn?"

"Oh, he's a genius," Mom says without missing a beat.

"A total galaxy brain," Carl says.

With that, the lens is back on me.

What should I say? I only know two things about Arlo Corn. One, he's the owner of Happy Town, both the company and the actual town. Two, he's a multi-billionaire. Should I admit that's all I know? Everyone seems to want me to say something else.

Mom and Carl are looking at me. The camera woman is looking at me. Her lens is looking at me. The camera woman clears her throat. "Keegan, your thoughts on Arlo Corn?"

I should just go with the flow.

"Arlo Corn is a genius," I say.

Grins. Thumbs. Nods.

The camera woman stows her camera away and brings out a pad. It's a contract for Mom and Carl to sign, something about giving Happy Town permission to use the video and our likenesses in any format, for any reason, forever.

They sign it, the camera woman moves on to the next new family, and we go inside our box.

Before I shut the door, I watch the blimp make another pass over the street. The mobile billboard glitches, the letters scrambling into visual noise.

"Hey, Mom . . . ?"

"Yeah?" she calls from the kitchen.

After a blink, the sign corrects itself, once more displaying the Happy Town slogan.

"Never mind."

TWO

The advertising blimp is back the next morning, displaying the weather report.

Seventy-four degrees, Fahrenheit.

Thirty percent humidity.

Chance of rain: zero.

Chance of snow: zero.

Chance of happiness: 100 percent.

All the zeroes are little pale-green happy faces.

The report switches to an ad for Sniffree. "Keep your family fresh with Sniffree body wash and you'll never have to sniff them again."

I take a nose sample of my armpits. The very last thing I want to do on my first day of school is be found sniffable.

A bread-loaf-shaped vehicle whispers up the street and stops at the corner where a cluster of other kids from the neighborhood wait. The vehicle—a "conveyor," as it's called in Happy Town—is my ride to school. I follow the others aboard and notice there's no driver in front, just a camera aimed at the passengers, who seem fairly quiet for a load of kids. Nobody's screaming. Nobody's throwing paper airplanes. Nobody's making goofy faces out the windows, and everyone's facing forward.

I claim an open seat and scoot over to the window. A girl drops herself next to me, and I'm about to say hello when she turns to a very large boy across the aisle.

"Hey, Tank."

The boy grunts and vaguely moves his hand. I don't think he's being unfriendly, just very absorbed in his book, a little paperback with a lot of pink and violet on the cover and a title written in red cursive.

"HEY, TANK," she tries again.

He blinks as if awakening to the world. "Oh, hi, Gloriana," he says with great cheer. Then he dives back into his book.

The conveyor sets off past the white, gray, and pale-green houses.

Sorry.

The *boxes*.

"Please sit back, relax, and enjoy our journey to school," says a perky recorded voice. "If you're new to Happy Town, welcome! Let's show you around. Look to your left and you'll spot the Fulfillment Center, where most of your parents work."

The Fulfillment Center is a concrete hockey puck, the same colors as all the rest of the buildings. Neither Mom nor Carl work there. Carl is an elevator mechanic who works all over the city. Mom is a thermal duct deployment manager, whatever that means.

"As you probably know, 'fulfillment' has different definitions. It can mean satisfaction or contentment. And it can also mean delivery of a product. That's what our Fulfillment Center does. It prepares products for delivery all over the globe, which makes people content. When you're older, maybe you'll get to fulfill the world's wishes and dreams."

"You new?" the girl next to me asks.

"How'd you know?"

"Most people in Happy Town are new. Plus, you're getting nose prints on the window."

I move my face away from the glass. "How long have you lived here?"

"Eight months. I'm an old-timer."

I start to ask her about life in Happy Town, but the conveyor speaks again. "Sasha, please put away your gum. Tank, please put away your book and pay attention."

A boy a few seats in front of me spits his gum into a wrapper, neatly folds it, and tucks it in his pocket.

Tank says "Unh" and gives a distracted wave. He turns a page.

The recording points out shops; offices; temples, mosques, and churches; elevated sidewalks connecting the high floors of the buildings; and MICE, the self-driving carts that zip out of holes in the streets and deliver groceries and household items throughout the city.

"The MICE network is a prototype of the delivery system Arlo Corn envisions in every city of the world. But it's only one of Arlo Corn's many innovations. Think of Happy Town as a laboratory where Arlo Corn's best ideas are tried out and perfected so they can be applied to other Happy Towns. Ours may be the first, but soon there'll be Happy Towns everywhere. Under the sea. In orbit. On the moon. And Mars. And one day, on planets across the universe!"

Gloriana snorts. I don't know what she finds snortworthy, but I decide to mind my own business and focus on the tour.

"As we pull into Happy Town Academy, we'd like to draw your attention to the heart and brain of our city, Corn Tower, where our founder Arlo Corn spends long hours planning for a future where all citizens prosper, where there is no poverty, no hunger, where every need is fulfilled."

I crane my neck to gaze up to the top of the white spire thrusting toward the sky. The only thing taller than Corn's office building is the clear glass dome that encases the entire city, protecting us from heat and cold and wind and rain, sealing us off from the rest of the world.

THREE

My social studies teacher is a tired-looking middle-aged man in a tweed blazer worn over a Happy Town T-shirt. He stares at an invisible spot in the air and twitches his fingers, as though he's typing. The electronic board behind him displays an ad for Meat Cramwich, the Microwaveable Meat Sandwich Crammed with Meat.

I take an open seat in the second-to-back row. This is a strategic decision. The first four rows are easily noticeable, and the back row is traditionally where troublemakers sit, at least at my previous schools. But the second-to-back row is sort of a netherworld for the very average, the boring, and the inconspicuous. The second-to-back row cracks no jokes, creates no distractions, does as instructed, goes with the flow.

My worktable is a panel of frosted white glass, and my fancy chair bristles with adjustment levers and knobs. I try to raise my seat and tilt the backrest forward, but I must be doing something wrong because all the levers are stuck in place.

The girl from the conveyor slips into the seat beside me.

"You're Gloriana. I'm—"

"Hold on," she says. "I have to do something before class starts."

From a transparent backpack she produces a coffee mug with the Happy Town logo. She places it on her worktable with care, turning it a little this way, a little that way, as if searching for some perfect position. Finally, she gives the mug a satisfied smile, then, like a cat, swipes it off the table. It hits the floor and shatters.

A few kids look over and whisper. The teacher continues to stare at nothing and phantom-type.

"What's your name?" Her face is friendly now, eyes warm.

"I'm Keegan. Why'd you do that?"

"It makes me feel better." She takes another mug from her bag and sets it in front of me. "You should try it."

If there's a nonjudgmental way to ask her exactly what kind of weirdo she is, I can't find it.

The teacher stops staring and twitching and addresses the class.

He says his name is Mr. Grossman, and it's time for a quiz.

Was I supposed to have learned something? School's only been in session five minutes. I don't even know where the bathrooms are.

My table lights up with a screen containing questions and a virtual keyboard and some buttons.

Gloriana's done with her quiz before I even get started.

It's a short quiz, all the questions about stuff covered in the tour. When I'm done I hit SUBMIT. My score comes back nine out of ten.

"I got a perfect score," Gloriana says, but it doesn't sound like bragging. More like she's disappointed. "How about you?"

"Nine. I missed the one on what MICE stands for."

"Mobile Intracity Delivery Express. Intracity is both the 'I' and the 'C.' The 'D' is silent."

We spend the rest of class reading from Arlo Corn's autobiography, *From Womb to Winner*. The first chapter covers his birth, at which apparently he did a great job.

After social studies comes math, then language arts. Neither are subjects I'm good at. I'm disappointed when I learn that art class is only once a week, on Fridays.

I find Gloriana again at lunch, and she shows me how to use a cafeteria kiosk to bring up a vast menu of options. There's nowhere to insert a money card or cash.

"You pay with your eye," she says.

"You what with your what?!"

"It's a retinal scan, see?" She leans in close to the kiosk with her left eye wide open. A little round camera flashes green and beeps. "They deduct the money from our parents' salaries. That's how everything in Happy Town gets paid for, from a juice box to a refrigerator. Delivery is included."

A segmented metal disk in the floor opens like a flower greeting the dawn, and little MICE crawl out of it, skittering all over the cafeteria floor and delivering orders of tacos and pizza slices and sandwiches and paper trays of chicken tenders.

Gloriana orders a rice bowl with a non-meat protein called "I Can't Believe It's Not Turkey," and then makes space for me at the kiosk.

I order a rice bowl with actual turkey and pay with my eye. Less than a minute later, a MICE rolls up to us bearing our bowls.

Amid chattering voices, I follow Gloriana outside to a long lunch table. The sun is bright, and the air is warm.

"I guess with the dome keeping the weather away we can eat outside every day. That's cool."

Gloriana grunts with a mouthful of rice. "I'm from Ohio," she says. "I don't miss snow, but I always liked the wet season. Everything gets mossy and mildewy."

"You miss mildew?"

"Sort of. It's gross, but at least it's natural. It's real."

I think I know what she means. I haven't seen a single bird since moving in. Not a pigeon. Not a sparrow. No bees. No butterflies. If I dug into dirt would I find ants? Is there even dirt in Happy Town?

"Okay, so really, why'd you break your mug?" I ask.

She chews. I can tell she's thinking. "I'll make a deal with you. If you can go a whole month without wanting to break a Happy Town mug, then I'll tell you."

"I don't think I'm going to want to break a mug." Breaking mugs in class is not the kind of thing a go-with-the-flow guy does.

Gloriana lets out a dry little laugh. "I'll keep bringing spares anyway. Just in case."

15

FOUR

I come home from school during "family hour," the brief window when Carl is home from his morning shift and Mom hasn't yet left for her night shift. This means an early dinner, and then I can go to my room and draw mammoths and dinosaurs and spaceships and ignore my homework if I have any, which I do not.

Carl presses buttons on the microwave while I join Mom setting the table.

"How was school?" she asks. "Were you social?"

"A little bit." The dinnerware is new, the spoons and forks and knives all embossed with the Happy Town logo. "I talked to a girl on the conveyor. She's in a couple of my classes."

"Is she pretty?" Carl asks in a teasing tone.

My eyes roll of their own accord. "I didn't check. She knocked a coffee mug off her desk in homeroom. On purpose. I think she may be a human-cat hybrid."

Mom puts out Happy Town drinking glasses and napkins. "She sounds like trouble."

"Nah, the teacher didn't even care. He was staring at nothing and pretending to type. Maybe it's all a Happy Town thing."

"Just please make good choices, Keegan."

"I will," I say with a little impatience, because I've made this promise at least a dozen times in the lead-up to the move here.

The microwave bings, and Carl plates up sandwiches with tall stacks of meat patties between shiny buns. He presents them like a chef debuting a new recipe. "What do you think?"

"They're very vertical."

"Right? This is Meat Cramwich, the Microwaveable Meat Sandwich Crammed with Meat. I saw an ad for them on a blimp and figured we'd give them a try. They came right to our door by MICE. Isn't that amazing?"

"But you're a vegetarian."

"Meat Cramwich, the Microwaveable Meat Sandwich Crammed with Meat, *is* vegetarian. Except for the meat."

He takes a big bite and makes happy eating noises.

I take a smaller bite.

Carl watches me expectantly.

"It's good," I assure him. "Real good." A more honest answer would be "It's not exactly delicious but the salt and fat make me want another bite."

Mom gives me a concerned-mom look. "You don't have to finish it if you don't like it."

"It's fine." I down another bite to show her how fine it is. "It's just . . . we usually have Indonesian food on Mondays."

My dad's Indonesian, and even after the divorce, even after Mom married Carl and we moved in with him, we kept up the dinner tradition.

Mom's eyes soften. I can tell she's frustrated with herself.

"You're right, Keegan. We haven't really been thinking about how hard this move was for you. We wanted to give you a better life, a better education, a better future, but that doesn't mean we have to leave everything behind."

"We'll do Indonesian tomorrow," Carl assures me.

"And then next week we'll move it back to Monday. Sound okay, kid?"

"It's fine," I say again, reminding myself of my plan to be a go-with-the-flow guy. And to prove how much I'm flowing, I gobble down the rest of my Meat Cramwich, the Microwaveable Meat Sandwich Crammed with Meat.

FIVE

If scientists invented flowers in a laboratory and came up with the scent by mixing and matching various chemicals until they discovered something that smelled like sugary cereal with hints of fruit syrup and a touch of nostril-stinging cleanliness, that's what my hair and body and hands would smell like.

Mom and Carl have stocked the bathroom and the kitchen with Sniffree, the soap I saw advertised on one of the blimps yesterday. The same ad is playing on the refrigerator screen as I eat a blueberry Happy Tart for breakfast.

Mom smells like Sniffree. Carl smells like Sniffree. The conveyor to school smells like Sniffree, except for a few kids who didn't wash and instead smell like dirty basketballs.

Gloriana smells like nothing in particular. Just like

yesterday, she sits next to me and says hello to the large boy across the aisle. Again, he's so lost in his book he barely responds, even when the conveyor voice tells him to put his book away.

I wonder why reading on the conveyor is against the rules. It must have to do with safety.

"Please sit back and relax and enjoy our journey to school," says the conveyor. "If you're new to Happy Town, welcome! Let's show you around. Look to your left and you'll spot the Fulfillment Center, where most of your parents work."

"Hey, Gloriana, can I ask you something?"

"Curiosity is dangerous, so go ahead."

"Are we caught in a time loop?"

"If we are, it has to be the kind where we're aware we're in a loop; otherwise it wouldn't have occurred to you that we're in a time loop."

I sit with that puzzle for a minute until my head starts to hurt. Meanwhile, the tour continues: "Think of Happy Town as a laboratory where Arlo Corn's best ideas are tried out and perfected so they can be applied to other Happy Towns. Ours may be the first, but soon there'll be Happy Towns everywhere."

"To answer your question, no, we're not in a time loop.

But, yes, it's the same tour every day. The same recording. It's a glitch and it's been this way since I moved here."

"Is it really that hard to fix?"

"You wouldn't think so."

"As we pull into Happy Town Academy, we'd like to draw your attention to the heart and brain of our city, Corn Tower, where our founder Arlo Corn spends long hours planning for a future where all citizens prosper, where there is no poverty, no hunger, and where every need is fulfilled."

"This is going to get on my nerves," I say.

"Well, look on the bright side. You'll be acing Mr. Grossman's quizzes for the rest of the year."

"Can I ask you something else? The conveyor . . . except for being driverless, and except for being outfitted with cameras . . ."

Gloriana nods, encouraging me to continue.

"Isn't it really just a bus?"

Gloriana puts a hand on each of my shoulders. She stares hard into my eyes. "Keegan," she says, "I'm going to tell you a very important truth about Happy Town. Are you listening?"

"You are very intense and it would be impossible not to."

"The conveyors are just buses. Understand that, and

you'll understand life under the dome."

With that, she goes on ahead of me to class, and I have no idea what to make of her revelation.

I'm relieved that, except for the quiz, social studies isn't an identical repeat of yesterday so I'm not actually caught in a time loop. Science-fiction stories are cool, but I don't want to live in one. The characters in those are always running for their lives, have no time for hobbies, and never get to go the bathroom.

Today, Mr. Grossman plays a video about how Arlo Corn built Happy Town with his bare hands (and six thousand construction workers) and invented the futuristic material the dome is made of.

Gloriana breaks another mug.

Kids glance over but quickly return their attention to the video. Mr. Grossman doesn't blink an eye. Like yesterday, he gazes off to nowhere and moves his fingers.

"What's he doing?" I whisper to Gloriana.

"Using his imp."

When she notices my blank stare, she says, "You know, his implant? The one all the adults in Happy Town have? No?"

I shake my head.

"Every Happy Town employee has an imp. It helps

them access data and send and receive messages and read, I dunno, columns and numbers. You know, work stuff."

"I don't think my mom and stepdad have them," I say slowly. "At least they've never told me about them. My mom's a thermal duct deployment manager, whatever that means. And Carl does something with elevators."

"If they work for Happy Town, they have imps. It's just a little earplug that attaches to neurons or ganglia or something. I don't know. I haven't ever seen what they look like from inside the head. Anyway, it goes in their ears and connects to their brains."

I cannot believe what I'm hearing. "Inside their heads?"

"That *is* where the brain is located in most people."

"Brain surgery? On their brains?"

"No, brain surgery on their butts."

"On their butts???"

Mr. Grossman clears his throat. "If we could have your attention, Gloriana and Keegan? We don't want to miss the part about how Mr. Corn started from nothing and built his fortune with hard work and big ideas."

"That, and his family's owned banks since the 1800s," Gloriana says in an obnoxious teacher's pet singsong.

The glare Mr. Grossman trains on her demonstrates that Gloriana is not, in fact, anything like a teacher's pet.

I try to pay attention to the video, but my thoughts storm with visions of Mom getting a secret cranial operation. It can't be true. She wouldn't do something so drastic just to get a job. And if she did, she'd tell me.

"DID YOU GUYS HAVE BRAIN SURGERY?"

Mom and Carl are watching the microwave spin.

Carl stares at the microwave door like a submariner looking for giant squid out a porthole. "Oh, hey, Keegan. We're having Indonesian tonight. It's Health-Fu, the Microwaveable Tofu Meal Crammed with Health."

"How is that Indonesian?"

"It's got an Indonesian Flavor Pack," Mom says.

"You can't just tear open a plastic bag and call it Indo . . . wait, don't distract me. Did you guys have brain surgery for your jobs?"

Mom laughs. "If we had brain surgery, don't you think we'd tell you?"

"Oh. Yeah. Of course you'd tell me."

My stormy head calms. My shoulders relax. I blow out a relieved breath. Gloriana was just messing with me. I've got to keep an eye on that. I don't want to get a reputation for being Gullible Kid.

Carl scratches behind his ear. "Where'd you get this

brain surgery idea from?"

"The girl I met, the destructive one, Gloriana. She said every adult has an implant installed in their head that connects to the Happy Town communication network. Something like that."

"Oh, are you talking about the imps?" Carl says. "Yeah, we all have them."

The head storm resumes. "How is that not brain surgery?"

"Brain surgery is when they use hammers and pliers to crack open your skull. This was more like getting contact lenses."

Mom gives me a reassuring motherly smile. "Really, the imps aren't a big deal. They're just tiny devices that help us do our jobs."

Carl gives me a reassuring stepfatherly smile. "They just dropped them in our ears with tweezers, and then the imps extended tiny little wires to wrap around our nerves."

"Our neurons, not our nerves," Mom corrects. "I'm sorry we didn't tell you, Keegan. We were all so busy with the move here that I guess we didn't get around to talking about it. Speaking of which . . ."

She goes to grab her hard hat and head out to work.

I eat my Health-Fu. The tofu tastes like a sponge. The Indonesian flavor pack tastes like hot glue.

Carl chews while phantom-typing.

Maybe I'm the one who had brain surgery and they removed the part that helps the world make sense.

SIX

Finally Friday. Art, the one class I've been looking forward to ever since I found out we were moving to Happy Town.

The classroom greets me with an electronic display board telling me to take any available seat, followed by an ad for breakfast cereal. This is the tidiest art room I've ever seen. Instead of paint-splattered desks and cabinets overflowing with construction paper and modeling clay and coffee cans full of stiff paint brushes, there are fancy office chairs and angled drawing boards with glass surfaces. Everything is white and gray, with occasional stripes of pale green.

Art is my favorite subject—the only subject I like,

actually—and when Mom and Carl told me about the move, they'd sold me on the amazing facilities and opportunities I'd have at Happy Town Academy. Looking over my art station, I feel they've fulfilled their promise. I envision months spent making pictures, drawing a comic book, maybe even making a short animated movie.

"Did you have art last year?" I ask Gloriana as she sets a coffee mug on the worktable next to mine.

"Nope. The art stations weren't hooked up yet."

"But you already have a mug ready. Seriously, why?"

"It's better to have a mug that you don't end up breaking than to need to break a mug and not have one."

"I'm not sure what that means, but witness me, I am going with the flow."

The teacher—Ms. Daemon—starts class with a cheerful bellow: "Good morning! Welcome to a brand-new year of artistic accomplishment!" Her blouse is a spatter pattern of bright colors, the frames of her glasses are fire-engine red, her hair has blue streaks, and her bright brown eyes shine with glee. I like loud, happy teachers. She goes over announcements and policies and procedures and class rules and gives us our first assignment: self-portraits showing ourselves doing what makes us happy.

As instructed, I find a stylus in a slot built into the art station. With a tap on the table surface, a whole collection of tools and colors appears on the screen. I select the pencil tool, adjust color and line thickness, and commence drawing myself in the act of drawing myself at the very art station I'm currently using. In my drawing of the art station screen, I will insert another picture of me drawing myself, and I'll continue until I run out of time or the drawings of me drawing are too small to make out.

I call upon every skill I've got—proportion and anatomy, perspective and foreshortening, stippling and crosshatching, and contours and lighting.

Forty minutes fly by. When Ms. Daemon says, "Styluses down, please," I've got something I'm really happy with.

Gloriana leans over for a look. "Wow, that's good!"

"Thanks! Can I see yours?"

"Sure."

She has drawn a stick figure walking away from a massive explosion.

"That's you?"

"Uh-huh."

"And the explosion?"

"That's the whole world."

"Cool."

"I want to thank you all for focusing on your assignment and maintaining a joyous creative environment," says Ms. Daemon. "Now, please remember to tap the 'submit' button before you shut down your stations."

Gloriana taps her finger on the screen. I do likewise.

A window pops up over my drawing. It's a long block of tiny text with a 'submit' button at the bottom. Considering how quickly the other students are tapping their screens and packing up their things, they must not be bothering to read the text.

"What's all this stuff say?" I ask Gloriana.

It's Ms. Daemon who answers. She stands over my shoulder. "It says 'submit.' Oh, and that's a terrific drawing, Keegan! Great work!"

"Thank you. But I mean all the writing. Do we have to read it?"

"It's just routine stuff," Ms. Daemon says, patient. "You can skip it and submit."

"Okay." I am happy to avoid a reading assignment, especially a long one in tiny text. I extend my pointer finger and bring it over the submit button when I catch something in the middle of the text block:

By submitting the academic assignment (herein referred to as The Work) the student grants Happy Town Academy and its parent corporation Happy Town Corporation exclusive rights of ownership, including but not limited to the rights required or necessary to publish, import, access, use, store, transmit, review, disclose, preserve, extract, modify, reproduce, share, use, display, copy, distribute, translate, and create derivative works from it, in print, electronic, audio, and all other technologies current or yet to be developed, in perpetuity.

"What's all this mean?"

"It means they own your school assignments," Gloriana says, hand on her mug.

"Like, my drawing? They own my drawing?"

"Yep."

"Thank you, Gloriana," says Ms. Daemon. "You'd better get to your next class."

She and Gloriana exchange tight-lipped smiles that don't seem very joyous. Gloriana zips her backpack with aching slowness, rises from her chair, and says, "See you Saturday, Keegan."

"What's on Saturday?"

Gloriana says no more and takes off.

She's left her mug behind.

Ms. Daemon adjusts her glasses. "Keegan, you also have a class to get to."

"But what if I want to keep my drawing?"

"It will be stored on the network. You can look at it whenever you want."

"But what if I want to print it out and put it on the refrigerator?"

"You can do that with Happy Town permission."

"I need permission to print out my own drawing?"

"Yes. But don't worry, we always grant permission for personal use."

"Personal . . . but it's *my* drawing." Gloriana's mug is starting to look tempting. "Why do I need permission for my own drawing that I drew myself of me drawing myself?"

Ms. Daemon clicks her tongue. "You used Happy Academy technology to perform the work. It only makes sense that Happy Town has ownership of it."

"But I didn't have a choice. There's no paper or paint or pencils—"

"If there were, they'd belong to Happy Academy."

"And this part about 'other technologies yet to be developed.' What if someone invents a device that makes it possible for people to electronically rip the image of my drawing right out of my brain and it gives me a hemorrhage and I die bleeding out my ears?"

"That is an absurd and impossible scenario."

"But what if?"

"Well, yes, Happy Town would own telepathic distribution of your work."

"What if I don't submit? Will you give me a zero?"

"Yes, and there would also be additional consequences."

Ms. Dameon's next class is already filing in. I don't want to be late to my own next class, which is math and I'm very bad at it and everybody's always saying "Math is a language" as if that's somehow supposed to make it easier.

"Just submit, Keegan."

Even though I'm bad at math and not great at writing and pretty bad at softball, my report cards always note that I'm a kind, courteous, and cooperative student. I've never gotten in trouble at school. No detentions, no letters sent home, no parent/teacher conferences about behavior. "There goes Keegan," my teachers would say to each other as I walked past. "What an obedient boy. Such a pleasure to have in class."

Ms. Daemon appears to take no pleasure in my presence.

"Submit, Keegan."

My finger reaches for the button. There's a teakettle screaming in my head. I hold my finger in check. Then move it forward a few millimeters closer to the button.

The kettle is about to explode.

"No."

"Excuse me?"

I pull my finger back. "I don't want Happy Academy to own my drawing."

"Is that your final decision? Think carefully, Keegan."

"It's my final decision." My voice squeaks a little.

"Then I'm happy to tell you you'll be attending Mandatory Work Opportunity at the Fulfillment Center this Saturday from 9 a.m. to 3 p.m. Pack a snack."

"Is that . . . is that detention?"

Ms. Daemon smiles brightly. "There is no detention in Happy Town. Now, onto your next class. And have a happy Saturday!"

I can't believe I'm in trouble. How can it be against the rules to say you don't want anyone else to own your art assignment? It's like letting someone own your thoughts.

I maintain a sullen silence on the ride home, barely looking at Gloriana. Instead, I stare out the window at the electronic billboards showing Arlo Corn's smiling face, and at the sprawling warehouse facilities, and at the dome trapping me inside like a fish in an aquarium.

SEVEN

Over an early dinner of some kind of salad product, I inform Mom and Carl about Mandatory Saturday Work Opportunity.

Mom's fork clinks on her plate. "You got detention?"

"There is no detention in Happy Town."

"Hmmph."

Carl watches the display screen built into the refrigerator, on which Arlo Corn is promoting all the fun weekend activities available in Happy Town, such as shopping from the comfort of one's sofa. "I think a work opportunity is a positive thing," Carl says. "School is great and all, but the stuff you learn in the real world is the most valuable education."

"School *is* the real world," I counter. "You're around

real people, doing real math and real reading and real whatever."

"But are you going to learn about elevator repair? Are they going to teach you thermal duct deployment management?"

"I actually don't know what thermal duct deployment means," I confess.

"It means the deployment of thermal ducts," Mom says with great dignity. "And I *did* learn it at school, thank you."

Carl coughs. "In any case, your conduct and achievement at school are subject to fines. If you get in trouble or don't perform well on exams, they can take money out of our paychecks."

My mouth falls open. "What? You're kidding."

"Nope. House rent and food and all the essentials we buy are deducted from our pay. Everything the MICE bring gets deducted from our pay. And your Mom and I have to pay fines if we're late to work or take long lunch breaks or don't get all the stuff done that we're supposed to. It's the same thing if you mess up at school. Not to put pressure on you."

"But I didn't mess up. I just didn't want to submit."

"We don't make up the laws, kiddo, but we must abide by them."

"How are these laws? I thought this was a free country."

"Technically they're not laws," Mom says. "They're company policies."

"You say to-MAY-to, I say to-MAW-to." Carl looks back at the fridge screen. It's playing an ad for marching band instruments.

"Do I have to go? It's a whole Saturday. I could be drawing in my room. Or getting to know the neighborhood kids, which is good for my social development, or exploring the town on my bike."

"You don't have a bike," Carl so helpfully points out.

"Maybe I could get one. I still have some birthday money. And a MICE could have it here in minutes."

"Two problems," Carl says. "Like I said, we pay for stuff directly from our paychecks. Your money is no good here."

"What's the second problem?"

"Bikes aren't allowed in Happy Town. They'd get in way of the MICE and they're a safety hazard and the hospital is still under construction."

I feel like I'm being boxed into a corner. My face is hot and my head is pulsing. I take three slow breaths until I trust myself to speak. If I haven't done anything wrong, why am I being punished? Why do I feel so guilty?

"What if I exchange my birthday money for Happy Bucks and pay the fine for skipping detention? Wouldn't that make everyone happy?"

Mom forks Happy Salad into her mouth. "There is no detention in Happy Town."

Later, when I'm up late, questioning the nature of justice and the universe and my value as a human being, Mom comes in my room. She's still wearing her reflective safety vest, and she's got hat hair from wearing her hard hat all night. She works hard. Carl does, too.

She sits on the edge of my bed. "I'm worried about you, kiddo."

"You don't have to be. I'm fine. It's just new-school stuff. There's a lot to get used to. And I'm sorry I got in trouble. Really."

She brushes a lock of hair out of my face. "You've always been my steady rock through rough waters. The divorce, starting a new phase of my life with Carl, all the moving around . . . I don't know what I would have done without you. But that's a lot of pressure to put on a kid, and it's not fair to you."

She's said this before. But what she doesn't seem to

realize is that I can handle the pressure. The divorce was a horrible, awful time. Mom was sad and scared. Dad was sad and scared. I was sad and scared, too, but I figured the best way to make things just ever so slightly less horrible and awful was to make as little trouble as possible. I didn't bother them with my own sadness and fear. I told them I was upset so they wouldn't worry about me locking away my feelings, but I didn't make a big deal out of it. I was helpful around the house. I didn't talk back or act out. I did what I was told at school and didn't get into any trouble.

"I like that you can count on me," I tell Mom. "And part of that is making sure you don't have to worry about me."

She laughs, tired. "I am always going to worry about you. It's in my mom contract."

"Well, trying not to get into trouble is in my kid contract. Next week I'm going to approach art class differently, and I promise."

She nods and kisses my forehead. "Thank you."

Morning rain flows in rivulets down the outside surface of the dome as I stumble off the conveyor and yawn through the entrance of the gargantuan Fulfillment Center. The rain doesn't strike ground inside the dome. There are no puddles in Happy Town.

I've decided to look forward to my Mandatory Saturday Work Opportunity, and the lobby is encouraging. A giant map winking with points of light shows everywhere a Happy Town package is being delivered in real time. The world swarms with glowing gnats. Other screens display behind-the-scenes views of the Fulfillment Center. Robotic arms load tall racks with merchandise. The racks propel themselves over vast floors in a complicated ballet and deliver themselves to workers in mech suits who transfer the items into shipping boxes and then place them on labyrinthine conveyor belts.

Maybe I'll get to wear a mech suit!

A man in a light-brown polo shirt and light-brown trousers with light-brown eyes and a light-brown mustache greets me. The employee ID hanging from a lanyard identifies him as Ed Brown, Senior Manager of Cardboard.

"You're late," says Ed Brown.

I turn to the clock on the wall. It says 7:56. "I was supposed to be here at 8:00."

"You were supposed to be at your workstation at 8:00."

"But . . . I don't know where my workstation is. This is my first day."

"That's why you should have gotten here at 7:45. If you're not early, you're late."

"I'm sorry."

Ed Brown does not express forgiveness. "Come with me. We're going to Box World."

Box World turns out to be a cavernous space with harsh lighting and a lot of cardboard. Towering shelves bear stacks of flat, unassembled boxes. Boxes speed along conveyor belts in an endless procession, and a platoon of workers stands shoulder to shoulder, hurrying to seal them with tape guns. They don't appear excessively happy. I'd go so far as to describe them as glum.

"Think of Happy Town Fulfillment Center as a human body," says Ed Brown, clearly reciting something he's memorized. "Box World is the heart. From here, the boxes continue on until arriving at their final destination, the customer. That makes this conveyor system the Fulfillment Center's esophagus."

I'm not sure I remember what the esophagus is. "That's the tube halfway between the stomach and the toilet?"

Ed Brown's mustache quivers.

Am I already in trouble? Note to self: Do not guess when it comes to bodily functions.

"Come with me," Ed Brown says, his voice tight.

He leads me along the twisty course of conveyor belts until we arrive at a chain-link steel cage the size of a basketball court. Inside the cage rises a wall of stacked boxes. Ed Brown brings me into the cage.

This isn't what I expected. I thought I'd be part of a group, a team, a crew. But it looks like I'll be alone. "Am I the only one with detention?"

Ed Brown glares.

"I mean, the only one with Mandatory Saturday Work Opportunity?"

"Of course not. There's labor to do all through the Fulfillment Center, and there are plenty of cages. Now, if you can withhold any more questions, we'll begin with a quiz. What is wrong with these boxes?"

A quiz? Oh, right, I'm on school time. "I see nothing wrong with the boxes." I doubt this is the right answer, but it's an honest one.

Ed Brown lets out a puff of breath in a way that says, "Oh, you hopeless, ignorant boy."

"The tape?" he prods.

I look more closely at the cardboard mountain. "Oh, the boxes are sealed but the tape is crooked." I'm embarrassed I hadn't noticed before, though to be fair to myself, the boxes and tape blend together in a beige visual desert.

"That's right. We refer to this phenomenon as 'substandard sealing.' You will serve Happy Town as a peeler. Your job is to peel the tape off. Later, the boxes will be returned to the box hub for reuse. Your quota is one box peeled every twenty-seven seconds. See the timer?" A clock wired to the cage counts down from twenty-seven. When it hits zero, it sounds an alarm like a nauseated rooster and the clock resets to twenty-seven seconds.

"Isn't there a machine that could do this?"

Ed Brown somehow manages to make his mustache frown. "You're a lot cheaper than a machine."

Considering I'm not getting paid, that's undoubtedly true. "Do I get a mech suit?"

"A peeler with a mech suit? Preposterous. One box peeled twenty-seven seconds. Got it?"

"Yes, sir." I almost salute, forgetting that a Senior Manager of Cardboard is a warehouse employee, not an army general.

Facing the wall of boxes, I have no idea where to start.

One box every twenty-seven seconds.

Twenty-seven seconds later, my fingers are ensnarled in

a strip of partially removed, extremely sticky tape.

"Don't panic!" bellows a voice. "I'm here to help!"

A large boy rushes out from behind the box wall. He holds a weathered paperback book, and I catch just a glimpse of cowboy and cowgirl and roses on the cover before it disappears in his back pocket.

"I'm Tank," he says, carefully freeing my fingers from the tape tangle. "You must be the new peeler."

"I'm Keegan. I've seen you on the bus. The conveyor is always telling you to put your book away."

"And I never will. So, first week at school and you already got detention? Tough break." I'm about to agree that, yes, it is a tough break, but Tank has more to say. "New kid in town, new place, new people. You don't know the backstory, the geography, the social dynamics. That's got to be rough." His eyes moisten with sympathy.

"It's not that bad. I mean I —"

"I will make sure you have friends." Tank tilts his head back and bellows, "GLORIANA, COME MEET OUR NEW BEST FRIEND."

Gloriana emerges from behind the box wall, her mouth smeared with dark-red fluid.

"This is Keegan," Tank says with a small bow and an

extravagant hand gesture. "Keegan, this is Gloriana."

"We already know each other," Gloriana says.

Tank is delighted. "Fantastic! We are now a trio of best friends."

I feel like I've been run over by a friendly truck. "Wow, that happened fast."

"Tank doesn't believe in the awkward getting-to-know-each-other phase of friendship. He just gets right to it."

"It's a life lesson," Tank says. "I got it from a book: *Inferno Hearts*. There's this guy, and he's a lawyer, and he works with this other lawyer, and they really like each other, I mean *like* like, but they don't get together until page two-fifty, which is okay because the plot's good, but . . ."

"Tank reads a romance novel every day. What are you up to now?"

"One-thousand four-hundred and sixty-two."

"He reads so fast he gets paper cuts."

I can see Gloriana's teeth when she speaks. They're smeared with the same red stuff that's on her face.

I have to ask. "Gloriana . . . is that blood?"

"Strawberry pancake syrup."

Glancing around, I see no sign of a pancake restaurant

or a pancake vending machine or pancakes. Which is a shame. Saturday mornings should be about pancakes, not cardboard boxes. "How'd it get on your face?"

"Funny thing, a whole carton of strawberry pancake syrup fell off a shelf and broke open and there was all this syrup and then somehow my finger ended up in it and then my finger somehow ended up in my mouth and then it kept happening."

Tank shoots her a disapproving look. "The carton fell? All by itself?"

Gloriana smirks. "Accidents happen."

I turn to the pile of poorly sealed boxes. "This is a lot of boxes. I guess we should get to work."

Twenty minutes later, I have a paltry number of unpeeled boxes and a hopeless tumbleweed of sticky tape. The clock timer continues to crow.

"Don't worry," Tanks says when he sees how crestfallen I am. "Nobody can do a box in twenty-seven seconds."

Gloriana agrees. "We should have told you before you started. The pace is designed for us to fail."

Tank and Gloriana have made even less progress than me.

"I don't understand."

"It's a Sisyphean task," Gloriana says. "You know, from Greek mythology?"

Is the sisyphean some kind of gland? "I don't know that one."

Tank helps remove a strip of tape stuck to the bottom of my shoe. "Sisyphus cheated death so the god of the underworld made him roll a boulder to the top of a mountain as punishment. But every time he got the boulder to the peak, it just rolled down the other side. And that's his life, rolling a rock uphill, back and forth, again and again, doomed to failure for all eternity."

"I still don't get it. What's the point?"

"The point is punishment." Gloriana says. "I only do it at all because I like the sound of tape ripping the cardboard."

"And I do it because Gloriana does it," Tank says. "We've been a duo for a long time."

"Three whole months," Gloriana says. "But we were missing a third, and three is the magic number for friendship and adventure."

They seem really happy to have me here. I wish I felt the same way. My cuticles are torn from rubbing them against the sharp edges of box lids. And there's tape gum residue between my fingers. I don't like being sticky. And I really, really don't want to get into even more trouble by not peeling my quota.

"We should probably get back to work. We're supposed to be learning about the real world of warehouse operations."

Tank finds this interesting. "Were you thinking of becoming a warehouse worker when you're grown up?"

I have to be honest. "Well, if I was, I'm definitely not anymore. What about you?"

"I don't know what job I'll have. I spend more time thinking about who I am instead of what I do."

"What's the difference?"

Tank settles in, pleased to explain. "Part of who you are comes from who your parents are, what they teach you, where you grow up, stuff that happens to you . . . but that's only part of it. The rest is up to you and the choices you make. Are you going to be the kind of person who helps other people when they're in trouble, or the kind who minds their own business? Are you going to accept things the way they are, or try to make them better? Are you going to fix broken things, even if it's not your fault they got broken? I don't know what kind job I'll have, but I'll be the kind of person who cares about other people's emotions."

Tank has clearly put an impressive amount of thought into this. "What about you, Gloriana?"

"I'll be happy doing anything as long as it's breaking stuff. Maybe I'll demolish buildings. Or did you know that big oil well fires are put out with dynamite?"

I have to confess that I did not know that, but it sounds like fun.

Tank tosses a box aside, not even bothering with the tape. "If you're not going to be a warehouse worker, then what?"

"I honestly don't know. I like to draw, but maybe I'd like it less if it was my job. And as for what kind of person I want to be . . ." I shrug. "I'd like to be one who doesn't get Mandatory Saturday Work Opportunity."

"Some people don't know who they are until they're forced to decide," Tank says. "Like when a bag of cash falls out of a bank truck. Or when they see a bunch of bullies picking on a kid. Or when a volcano erupts and they're the only ones with lava boots."

"Well, I'm going to vote for a bag of cash and against a volcanic eruption," says Gloriana. "Besides, lava boots aren't a thing."

When 3 p.m. finally arrives, Ed Brown is nowhere to be found. I follow Tank and Gloriana from the cage, which still contains a mountain of boxes and now a floor covered in a foot of knotted tape.

On the way out, we pass workers loading MICE with cartons of band instruments.

The big screen in the Fulfillment Center lobby is playing a new ad, this one starring a man in a straw hat and bowtie. "America," he says, "we got trouble. Oh, we got trouble." He goes on to describe this trouble in exacting detail. It has something to do with the dangerous decay of civilized behavior. The decline of the human species. Everyone is threatened, but mostly the youth of America.

The answer to these troubles, he claims, is marching band instruments.

EIGHT

"Hey, you guys, I'm home. I made some friends at the Fulfillment—"

BLAAAAAAAATTT.

"What the —?"

BLAAAAAAAATTT. BLAAAAAAAATTT.

The *blaaaaaaaattt*s sounds like a whale in distress, loud enough to rattle the windows.

Has Carl been eating beans?

BLOOOOOOOOOOOTTTT. BROOOOOOOONK BROOOOOOOOOONK PHOOOOOOOOT.

The noises are coming from the backyard, and there's no scenario in which this is good news.

Phoot, Phoot, BROOOOONK.

Reluctantly, I go to investigate. When I get to the sliding patio doors, my brain struggles to make sense of what I'm witnessing: Carl is wrestling a metallic monster, a golden serpent entwined around his torso.

He spots me through the glass doors and waves.

No, not a monster. It's a tuba. Carl is in possession of a tuba, and he's trying to play it. This means Carl is the monster. A monster with a marching band instrument.

FLARRRRRRRP.

I slide the door open, brave the backyard. "Carl. Why did you buy a tuba?"

"Actually, it's a sousaphone. Common mistake. But notice the resonant lacquered brass body and twenty-six-inch horn for dynamic bombasity. And check out these stainless steel valves. They provide nimble playability and resistance to saliva-based bacterial accumulations! Listen!"

BLOOOOOOT BLOOOOT BLOOOOOOT.

I stick my fingers in my ears. "Is Mom home?"

"Upstairs." *BROONK POOOOP.*

I shut the patio doors and escape up the stairs, expecting to find Mom hiding from the noise in her home office.

"Hey, Mom, do you know what's up—"

WAH-WOMP.

Oh. No.

My mother has a trombone.

"May I go to my friend's house, please?"

WOMP-WOMP.

The walk to Tank's house sounds like a parade. Blasts and toots and piercing tweets come from the houses. MICE laden with boxes scurry in the streets to deliver yet more implements of sonic doom. I find Tank and Gloriana sitting on Tank's front steps. As evening falls outside the dome, the atmosphere inside is dry and warm, exactly as it had been this morning and all through the day. I miss the sounds of crickets and bullfrogs from the drainage canal that ran behind our apartment in San Diego.

"What's September like where you're from?" I ask my new friends.

"The nights are still hot, but it'll start cooling off soon," Gloriana says. "And the cicadas will be screeching. Sometimes I screech back at them."

Tank smiles as if thinking of a fond memory. "I grew up in LA. I could hear the freeway from the apartment. It sounded like the ocean. It relaxed me."

A blimp lumbers overhead like a floating hippo. It's

playing the ad I saw in the Fulfillment Center lobby with the man in the straw hat claiming band instruments are the cure for all society's ills.

A thunderous *WOOOM BWOOOM BWOOOM* reverberates inside Tank's house.

Tank tilts his blood-drained face toward the sky. "How can this be allowed?" he wails. "What kind of universe tolerates this?"

BWOOOM BWOOOM answers the universe.

"Bass drum," Gloriana explains.

"Yeah, that's bad," I say. "My mom has a trombone. My stepdad has a tuba. Sorry, it's actually a sousaphone. Common mistake. Any music-related weirdness going on at your house, Gloriana?"

"My mom bought an impeccably crafted flute with a high-polish sterling silver body and a rose gold lip plate."

"This is weird, right? This isn't just a normal Happy Town thing?"

"Yes, very weird," confirms Tank.

"So what are we going to do about it?"

Gloriana shoots to her feet. "I'm going to drown my sorrows in a Slurry. Who's with me?"

Slurry Spigot Station is almost a mile away, and by the

time we get there on foot, the horrific symphony has faded behind us. In this neighborhood, a circling blimp plays an ad for running shoes. "Don't run away," says the ad. "Run toward." MICE zip from house to house, dropping off shoeboxes. At least running shoes are quiet.

"Why do people want something just because they see an advertisement for it?"

Tank answers my question: "It's not about wanting a shoe or a saxophone. It's about wanting to feel included, or cool, or happy. It's about wanting to see yourself as a certain kind of person: adventurous, or smart, or rebellious, special in some way while also fitting in. Advertising works by linking those emotions to a product."

"Wow, you know a lot about advertising."

"I learned it from a romance book. He's a former millionaire who's given away all his worldly possessions and lives in a yurt in the woods. She's president of the biggest ad agency in New York. It was called *Love and Adversity*."

Slurry Spigot Station turns out to be a squat gray shop a few blocks from the residential streets. Along the back wall stretch rows of cup dispensers and an illuminated menu of Slurry choices. As far as I can tell, Slurries are beverages.

The shop is quiet, just me and my friends, a few adults in

new clean sneakers, and some random kids who exchange nods with me and Tank and Gloriana. I don't see any Spigot employees.

"I'm getting chocolate," announces Tank. He eye-pays and grabs a cup.

Gloriana does the same thing.

I usually walk around with a few dollars in my pocket for emergencies, plus whatever I earn from mowing lawns, but I'm pretty sure all the grass in Happy Town is artificial, and nobody here takes cash anyway. I hesitate at the retinal scanner for a second, wondering if it's okay to use my parents' money without their permission. But my ears are still ringing from their most recent purchases, and I feel I'm owed a Slurry.

I eye-pay and grab a cup. The menu is a complex maze of screens and options, and I decide to hurry up and select something before I drown in a sea of too many choices. I pick banana-strawberry.

"That's a good one," Tank says, laboring to suck up brown goop through his straw.

The machine hums. It dribbles like a sloppy baby into my cup for a few seconds, then makes a choking noise, and dribbles no more.

"Hey," says a woman a few spigots down. She also gets dribble. In fact, all the spigots seem broken, and the Slurry shop fills with murmurs of disappointment, complaints, and some cussing.

A recorded voice intones, "Please wait and remain happy. Help is on the way."

The message repeats, over and over, and after a couple of minutes, I begin to suspect that help is not, in fact, on the way. I do make an attempt to remain happy.

Gloriana grabs another straw. "Here," she says. "We can share. I got berry."

"Thank you!" I take a sip. It tastes like purple.

"You can have some of mine, too," offers Tank.

Passing cups back and forth, we start for home.

Behind us, the recording continues:

Please wait and remain happy. Help is on the way.

Please wait and remain happy. Help is on the way.

Please wait and remain happy. Help is on the way.

NINE

Monday: I take Mr. Grossman's quiz and ace it thanks to the conveyor's endless repeat of the Happy Town tour.

In math, we go over factors of ten.

A one followed by a zero is ten.

Got it.

A one followed by two zeroes is one hundred.

Okay so far.

A one followed by three zeroes is one thousand.

I'm doing great.

And I'm still good with four zeroes and five zeroes and six zeroes.

It's when we get to nine zeroes that I start to freak out. A billion is easy to say, but my brain isn't equipped to fully comprehend how much that is. But since Mom and Carl can get fined if I get bad grades, I'm determined to figure it out.

One billion is equal to one thousand million.

Nope, still don't get it.

Let's try working it out practically.

If you started earning a million dollars every year from the day you were born, you would have to have been born a thousand years ago to have a billion dollars today. That's back before the invention of the flush toilet. You'd be pooping in a hole.

Arlo Corn doesn't have a billion dollars. He has six hundred and forty billion dollars. To be as rich as him, you'd have to earn a million a day starting from before the invention of toilet paper.

"This can't be right," I mutter.

Ms. deConsolable comes over to my table. "What can't be right, Keegan?"

I show her my work on the screen.

She gives me an approving smile. "You're absolutely correct. And when you think about it, it must mean Arlo Corn works billions of times harder and is billion of times smarter than your average person. Good work, Keegan!"

Good work! I did good work! That's the kind of thing adults tell you when you are going with the flow. And, man, am I flowing.

A girl named Sonya raises her hand. "I heard Arlo Corn was born a multi-millionaire because his parents and his grandparents and his great-grandparents were already rich, so maybe he's not all that smart and doesn't work all that hard."

The class grows uneasily silent. A cloud of dread settles over us. You'd think Sonya had just called Ms. deConsolable a dirty name.

"Why, Sonya, that's a very interesting thought," Ms. deConsolable says, air-typing with her imp.

Sonya's shoulders slump. She knows she screwed up. "Saturday Mandatory Work Opportunity?"

"Yes, and you'll be learning waste receptacle hygiene."

"Scrubbing toilets?"

"Mm-hmm," Ms. deConsolable says cheerfully.

So I've learned two things today:

1. How much a billion is.
2. Again, what happens when you go against the flow in Happy Town.

Tuesday: The neighborhood blimp plays the running

shoe ad ("Don't run away, run toward"), and there are running shoes waiting for me when I get home, and soon my feet are empillowed in new running shoes. I can't think of anything I want to run toward.

Wednesday: Tank confides that he smuggled in most of his books when he moved to Happy Town. He tells me some of them are banned in Happy Town for dangerous content, though they all seem to me like sappy stories about people falling in love.

Thursday: Carl complains of a high-pitched noise in his ear, so he goes to the Happy Town clinic to have his implant checked out. Turns out his imp is fine, but he sustained temporary hearing damage from playing his sousaphone. Mom also goes in for a high-pitched noise. They tell her it's due to noisy machinery in the thermal ducts and advise her to remember to wear ear protection, which she always does.

Friday: I come prepared for art.

I bring my own pencils.

I bring my own markers.

I bring my own paper.

"Nice sharp pencils," Gloriana says, admiring them. "I bet you could really stab someone with those."

"Or I could just draw with them."

"Enh. Where'd you get 'em? They're not Happy Town branded."

"My dad sent them for my birthday last year. He's a cook on a cruise ship, so I don't see him much. But he worked out a deal so I can spend next summer sailing with him."

"That sounds cool. Sometimes I forget there's a whole world outside the dome."

"Today we're doing an imagination study," Ms. Daemon announces. "I challenge you to draw a tree based on your idea of what a tree might look like if it weren't constrained to reality. Please open your Happy Art Palette and begin."

"Not this time," I mutter. There aren't many trees in Happy Town, mostly a few palms, some spindly palo verdes, and things that aren't really trees, like cactuses. But the assignment is to use my imagination, so I envision a tree the size of a mountain, the top poking through the clouds. And maybe a volcano? Yes. I will draw a giant volcano-tree spewing lava and sap.

I array my tools on the work surface and sketch lightly in pencil.

Gloriana's using her Happy Palette to draw an explosion. It's not clear what's exploding, but it's a very big explosion.

"Aren't you going to do the tree assignment?"

"Nope."

"But you're going to get detention again."

"There is no detention in Happy Town."

I'm determined to avoid another Saturday in the box cage, so I focus on my tree. For the next half hour, I work on billowing smoke and high flames and residents of the city at the foot of the volcano running in terror.

"Oh, Keegan, that's beautiful!"

Ms. Daemon looks over my shoulder. "I love the vibrant colors. And the way your reds and purples swirl with energy. And the fear in the eyes of the victims is convincingly rendered."

"I was thinking of setting some of the victims on fire. Too much?"

"Maybe a little. So what are you planning to do with this drawing?"

"Um. Turn it in?"

She smiles like a snake about to snap its jaws around a mouse. "Do you know how to use Happy Palette to scan it? See, you just put your drawing face down on the table and click the camera button. Go ahead, Keegan. Scan your drawing."

"Can't I just hand it to you?"

"If you did that, how would we share it? Wouldn't it be selfish to keep such a good drawing to yourself? Sharing is happiness, and Happy Palette makes sharing easy."

"Maybe I could just pin it to the wall? People could come by and look at it if they want."

"Happy Palette," Ms. Daemon says firmly.

"Uuugggh," I argue.

"Are you going to cooperate?"

"Probably not."

"Do you know what this means?"

"Mandatory Work Opportunity?"

"Indeed."

"Saturday at 8:00 meaning 7:45?"

"No, I'm giving you Mandatory Friday Work Opportunity, today at 4:00 meaning 3:45."

Once Ms. Daemon moves along, Gloriana offers me a Happy Town mug to smash.

I am tempted.

Associate Manager of Cardboard Ed Brown greets the three of us with a disappointed mustache.

"Wasn't he Senior Manager before?" I whisper to Tank and Gloriana.

"My parents get demotions and pay cuts all the time,"

Tank says. "It's supposed to keep the employees motivated. When I started here he was Ed Brown, Senior Director of Cardboard. He was less involved with sticky tape back then."

Ed Brown, former Senior Director of Cardboard, leads us past additional cages where kids peel tape off boxes or apply tape to boxes or struggle to straighten out hopeless tape tangles. In other cages, adult workers pick items from racks of products, put them in boxes, and cart the boxes to various conveyor belts.

Our assigned cage is stacked with toaster-sized boxes, thousands of them spread across the floor and towering all the way up to the chain-link mesh ceiling. Ed Brown tears one open with a razor blade, reaches in, and withdraws a fuzzy tiger. "This is an Automal," he says. "And it is mired in malfunction."

"That means it doesn't work," Tank translates.

"Please do not interrupt again or I'll have to dock your wages."

"How much money are we making, anyway?" I ask.

"Less now." Ed Brown clears his throat before continuing. "Due to a design flaw that is entirely not Happy Town's fault, Automals deliver a nonfatal but quite painful electrical shock to customers. As a precaution, we've had other

67

Mandatory Work Opportunity students drain their batteries and reseal them in their boxes. Your job is to unseal the boxes and recharge the batteries, then return them to their boxes and reseal them. Don't turn the Automals on unless you want to zap yourselves. Are there any questions?" He glares in a way that invites no questions.

I raise my hand.

"Yes?" Ed Brown says with a sigh.

"I just . . . I'm trying to . . ."

Ed Brown taps his foot.

"Just . . . why? If they electrically shock people, why are we recharging the batteries? Why are we putting them back in boxes?"

"Arlo Corn is a genius, and he found a place to sell them where you're allowed to electrify people. Thus ends our question-and-answer period. Please get to work. I'll leave you to it."

On a plastic folding table sits a black plastic brick with charging ports and a few box cutters. Gloriana grabs one and flicks the blade open. "I'll cut open the boxes. You two can recharge the tigers and beavers and skunks and whatever."

"Is this so you can play with sharp objects?" asks Tank.

"Of course." Gloriana starts slicing. She makes

aggressive noises like "grargh" and "grrr" and occasionally says things like "Die, box, die!"

I survey the mountain of boxes. "There must be thousands of these. We could spend our whole lives doing this."

"Roll that stone, Sisyphus." Tank plugs a fuzzy crocodile into the charging brick. I plug in an aardvark. "Gloriana said you tried to outsmart Ms. Daemon with art supplies."

"And now I'm paying the price. What was your crime?"

"Same thing as every other time: reading a book on the conveyor."

"Why is that a bad thing? Why do they care?"

"Well, when you read it means you're looking down, and anyone seeing you through the window might think you're not happy."

"Are you happy on the conveyor?"

"Sometimes, yes. Sometimes, no."

"There is no unhappiness in Happy Town," Gloriana says, stabbing another box.

I plug in an ocelot. "I guess I don't have to ask why you get so much work opportunity."

"It's not what you think. My mom has diabetes. She's okay if she gets insulin, but it's expensive, so we're in debt to Happy Town."

"Your mom needs medicine so *you* have to work? That

doesn't seem fair. That's even worse than punishing me for not cooperating in art class."

Go with the flow, I remind myself. Even if it seems to be heading for a waterfall.

After a few hours of repetitive tasks and hypnotic noise from endless commercials playing on the display boards, I lose track of time. When I look up from my work, a lot of the surrounding cages are empty. But only the ones that had been occupied by adult workers.

"Hey, you notice anything weird?"

"I try not to," Gloriana says, slicing tape like an assassin. "I get less upset that way."

"No, Keegan's right," Tank says. "Where'd the adults go? Actually, this reminds me of *Phantom Affection*. He runs a bed and breakfast. She's one of his guests, and she's a quantum inventor, and every time he's ready to confess his love she gets yanked into another dimension where she's fallen for another quantum inventor. It gets pretty complicated from there."

I wouldn't mind if Ed Brown got sucked into another dimension. But here he comes, walking down the row between cages with a sandwich in hand. I glance at the nearest display board. The Meat Cramwich ad is playing. I look at Ed Brown's sandwich. Then back at the Meat Cramwich ad.

"Good sandwich?" I ask.

"It's not a sandwich. It's Meat Cramwich, the—"

"The Microwaveable Meat Sandwich Crammed With Meat."

"It is a sandwich," says Gloriana. "It's right there in the name."

Ed Brown chews. "Don't interrupt me again or I'll dock your pay. Now please get back to work." His mouth is full of meat, so it sounds like "Don rupp megain er I'll dogyerbay now pleeb gedbackgoowork."

Tank and Gloriana and I gedbackgoowork.

Gradually, the adult workers stream back into their cages and they, too, gedbackgoowork.

Each of them is gobbling a Meat Cramwich.

The ad changes on the electronic display.

Now it's an ad for hats.

Just as they had returned to their cages, the workers leave them again like a line of ants marching to a picnic.

They come back wearing hats.

TEN

Monday again, lunchtime, and the line at the ordering kiosk moves at the pace hair grows. Gloriana and I are stuck at the back, and at this rate, I'm afraid I'll have to get through the rest of the day fueled on nothing but disappointment.

"What's the holdup?" Gloriana calls to the front of the line. The lack of tacos has made her crabby.

"There aren't any food options," the kid at the front calls back. "But if you ever wanted a lawn mower, this is the time."

"Do they have the kind you can ride?"

The kid consults the kiosk. "Nope."

"What's the point of a lawn mower you can't drive over stuff with," Gloriana grumbles.

I hope this glitch isn't like the Slurry Spigot situation. All I had for breakfast was a Meat Cramwich the Microwaveable Meat Sandwich Crammed with Meat, and I need a pizza slice to settle my stomach.

Alas, all the kiosks do is repeat the same message:

Please wait and remain happy. Help is on the way.

Later that afternoon in math class, we're supposed to be learning about converting fractions to decimals and vice versa and I don't know why society doesn't decide on one or the other. But when the bell signals the start of the period, Ms. deConsolable hasn't shown up.

After five minutes go by, we start to form theories:

She got demoted.

She's been fired.

She's fallen in a hole.

She was eaten by bats, even though there are no bats in Happy Town, as far as I know, and even if there were, I don't think they eat math teachers.

Me, I just figure she's spending time in the bathroom. Bathroom issues take precedence over chiming bells.

But when ten minutes have passed, Jed Tart, who is good at basketball and is therefore popular, announces he's done waiting. He gets up from his workstation and walks right out of the room. Other kids follow him, and after another ten minutes, I find myself alone in an empty classroom.

The hall is full of kids meandering and gossiping. Apparently *all* the teachers are missing.

I find Gloriana and Tank conferring outside the teachers' lounge.

"I wonder if this is one of those stories where all the adults vanish and the kids have to figure out what's going on?" Gloriana muses.

"I like those kind of stories," I say, "but I think this is something else." I point to the sky. The ad blimp circles overhead. It's playing the hat ad.

We all nod.

There's no point in denying the obvious truth about what's happening.

The teachers have all gone to buy hats.

The teachers all have implants.

All the adults in Happy Town have implants.

The implants and Happy Town advertisements are turning the adults into product-buying zombies.

At home the living room floor is strewn with open boxes and bubble wrap like the guts of a slain prey animal. Piles of hats cover the kitchen table: berets, boaters, bonnets, bowlers, fezzes, chef's toques, deerstalkers, ten-gallons, derbies, a pith helmet.

The ad for hats loops on the TV and the refrigerator screen.

I text my friends. "Hats?"

"Lots of hats," Gloriana texts back.

"So very many hats," texts Tank.

"Oh, hi," my mom says, coming into the room. "Want a hat?"

"No thank you." My words are short and tense.

Mom sports a red cowboy hat with white fringe around the brim.

She blinks, confused. "Really? Why not? I think you'd look cute in a beanie." She digs through boxes, searching. "Here it is. Oh, wait, this is a fruit hat. Such great bananas and pineapples." She holds it out in offering.

I can no longer go with this flow. This flow is too weird.

"I DO NOT WANT A HAT!" I roar. "I WANT YOU TO REMOVE YOUR IMP! AND STOP LOOKING AT SCREENS!"

"Why would we do that?" Carl asks, coming from the

bathroom. He's sporting a fedora with a red feather tucked in the band.

"*Why??* Because . . . hats . . . tubas . . . Meat Cramwich . . ."

"Sousaphones," Carl corrects me.

"AAAUGHHHHHHGUUUUGHH!" I rebut.

The hat advertisement on the screens is replaced by smiling, happy people. They're eating sandwiches.

"Meat Cramwich," says a smiling, happy woman. "The Microwaveable Meat Sandwich Crammed—"

I grab the remote and switch off the TV. But the voice continues from the kitchen. "—with Meat!"

Mom regards a giant floppy straw hat, then puts it down. "Hey, you know what would be great right now?"

Carl stops struggling to fit the fruit hat over his too-large head. "Are you thinking what I'm thinking?"

"Meat Cramwiches for dinner?" says Mom.

Carl looks out at nothing in particular and phantom-types. "Done!"

"Are you sure you ordered enough?" Mom asks, looking more worried than the time I developed a 103-degree fever and broke out in a purple rash.

"I ordered twelve," Carl assures.

"Is twelve enough?"

"Twelve cases. That's one hundred and forty-four Meat Cramwiches, the Microwaveable Meat Sandwich Crammed with Meat."

My phone shudders. It's Gloriana. "Meet on the corner. Now."

"I think you mean 'meat' at the corner," I almost type back, but this isn't the time for jokes.

Several blocks down the street, Tank sits on the curb in front of his house, reading a paperback. The cover features a pair of chefs embracing in a restaurant kitchen over a steaming kettle of soup. The title is *Hungry Hearts*.

Gloriana chucks rocks at passing MICE.

"Meat Cramwich situation at your houses?" I ask.

Gloriana throws more rocks. They ping off the MICE, leaving scratches and dents. "My mom was salivating. There was actual drool on her actual chin."

Tank flips a page of his book. "My dad's not even waiting for them to defrost. He'll be lucky if he doesn't break his teeth."

"We can't let our parents drool and break their teeth," I declare. "We all know what's going on, right?"

"Advertisements working with implants to make all

the adults in town lose their minds and buy whatever the screens tell them to?"

"It sounds out there when you say it aloud, but I'm pretty sure you just nailed it. The question is what are we going to do about it?"

Gloriana produces a Happy Town mug.

"Breaking stuff isn't the answer to everything."

Gloriana makes a doubtful noise but stashes the mug away.

Tank turns another page with a thoughtful expression. "I have an idea. In my book the chefs are in love but they keep fighting over the soup du jour recipe. Eventually they take their complaints to the restaurant owner, who turns out to be a really good matchmaker, and she forces them to collaborate on a new soup and their soup wins awards and they get engaged and live happily ever after."

"I don't like soup," Gloriana says with contempt.

Tank is mortally offended. "How can you not like soup? Soup is all the different food, just in soup form."

"Food should not be liquid. Beverages are liquid."

"It's not really about soup—" Tank says, defensive.

"It's about solving a problem by going to the person in charge," I interrupt. My gaze turns toward the center of town, where the white tower rises high above the other buildings, to the peak of the dome. The windows of the highest floor glint in the sun like gold. "Let's go see the genius."

ELEVEN

The Corn Tower lobby sparkles white and spotless, a place where germs go to die. A long reception desk floats like a white island in a sea of white floor tiles. Dressed in white coveralls, a custodian polishes a looming statue of Arlo Corn as tall as an apatosaurus skeleton in a museum. Made of blinding bright chrome, it has eight arms and it's squeezing a globe as if performing the Heimlich maneuver on the Earth.

Screens above a bank of elevators display the Meat Cramwich ad.

"I thought there'd be a lot of security," says Gloriana.

Tank pokes the white leaf of a white plotted plant. "Maybe they're in white camouflage so we can't see them."

I march up to the reception desk. "We'd like to see Arlo Corn, please."

The receptionist wears a tight-lipped smile. "School field trips are held in February and are open to all students who have accumulated sufficient productivity credits."

"You don't understand, we are here on *urgent business*."

The smile pulls tighter. "Children with *urgent business* are seen on Activist Thursday in the third week of May. We provide lunch."

"Lunch is kind of the problem."

A woman in a security guard uniform approaches the receptionist. A single spot of red sauce mars her otherwise pristine white shirt. "Is there something wrong with your imp?" she asks the receptionist. "Didn't you see the announcement?"

"I've been distracted by this band of plucky youths."

The security guard barely spares us a glance. "Well, we've got Meat Cramwiches in the break room. Better hurry if you want one; they're going fast."

The receptionist leaps from her chair with enough speed to leave Earth orbit and charges off with the security guard.

I wish I could take satisfaction in having my imp/advertising theory all but proven. "Well, here we are, all alone."

"Alone means unsupervised," says Gloriana. "Let's find Arlo's office."

She presses the elevator UP button. A moment later the doors open and three teenagers spill out.

"Oh, look, it's another band of plucky youths," says one of them, their silver nose ring gleaming in the lobby lights.

"We are not a band of plucky youths," Gloriana protests.

Tank puts a comforting hand on her shoulder. "I'm pretty sure that's exactly what we are."

Another teen speaks, this one in an Anarchy Now T-shirt. "There're multiple bands of plucky youths in Happy Town trying to do something about the implants and the out-of-control consumer cravings."

"Oh, see, we think that's what's going on, too." Having older kids agree with our theory is comforting. Maybe we don't have to tackle all this . . . what, strangeness? Disturbing phenomena? Weird disastery-feeling . . . stuff . . . on our own.

"Were you planning to go up and talk to the boss?" says Nose Ring. "You can forget it. It's chaos up there."

I try to ignore their discouragement. "But you saw Arlo Corn? You talked to him?"

"It wasn't much of a conversation," the third teen says, looking comfortable in pink pajama pants. "He just babbled about immortality and severed heads and rocketry."

"Also ladders and helicopters," says Anarchy Now.

"So, what do we do?"

"We?" scoffs Nose Ring. "*We* are getting out of town as fast as we can, and if you're smart, you'll do the same."

Oh.

Teenagers. They're not as bad as adults, but they get closer every day.

I turn to Tank and Gloriana "Are we smart?"

"Heck no," Gloriana says as though the very notion is preposterous. Except she doesn't actually say "Heck."

We pile into the elevator, and I jab the button for the highest floor.

Pink Pajamas gives us a sympathetic look. "Watch out for the zombie cannibals," he says.

"Ha ha?" Tank responds with a hopeful question mark.

The doors slide shut, and the elevator ascends so fast my ears pop. A display screen over the buttons counts the floors until being interrupted by a Meat Cramwich ad. This one comes with a jaunty jingle: "Meat Cramwich, the sandwich crammed with meat, microwaveable for a meaty treat."

"We're all still normal, right?" Gloriana asks. "None of us want a Meat Cramwich?"

The very thought makes me queasy. "I'm contemplating never eating again."

Tank frowns, concerned. "But you'd die."

"Not necessarily. My strong revulsion might keep me going."

"I wonder what he's like," Tank says, watching the floor numbers go up.

Gloriana also watches the numbers. "Arlo Corn? I don't know. I've never met a billionaire genius before. I bet he's got laser goggles."

"What about rocket boots?" Tank says. "Or an internet helmet? What do you think, Keegan?"

"I think he'll have robots picking up his trash and feeding him caviar."

"I bet he eats hummingbird tongues," Tanks says, and then he goes on to tell us about a banquet scene in a romance novel set in ancient Rome, which is where the word "romance" comes from.

Minutes later, the elevator delivers us to a palatial office. An entire wall made of a single pane of glass offers a commanding view of Happy Town. Even the second-tallest building, the hospital, seems tiny and very far down. Near the top of the dome lumbers an advertising blimp. Is it playing the Meat Cramwich ad? Yes, it is playing the Meat Cramwich ad.

More than the size and the view, what impresses me most about Arlo Corn's office is the sense of chaos and stink. Fragments of smashed computers litter the floor, along with the confetti of shredded documents. A pungent smell stings my nostrils. The source is a steel barrel stenciled with the words "HYDROCHLORIC ACID—CAUTION— HIGHLY CORROSIVE."

Arlo Corn is scooping up smashed computer parts and dropping them in the barrel. He's not wearing laser glasses or rocket boots or an internet helmet. Nor does he command an army of robot servants. He's just a guy in a Happy Town polo shirt, shorts, and flip-flops. His forearms are big and so is his head, but he basically looks like a regular guy.

He wipes a forearm across his sweaty forehead. "Wallace," he bellows. "Why do you keep letting plucky youths into my office?"

A man in a baby-blue sweater is on his knees, feeding paper into a shredder. "I'm sorry, Mr. Corn, I keep getting distracted by my insatiable craving for meat."

"I need you to concentrate, Wallace. Can you do that?"

Wallace confirms that he can with a shuddery nod. He shoves more paper into the shredder. Saliva gleams on his chin. "It's just that I wish I had meat."

Corn checks his watch and spends a few seconds staring at the ceiling. "Wallace, I'd appreciate it if you could be a happy personal assistant and show our young guests who do not have an appointment out the door?"

Wallace gets to his feet. His eyes land on the three of us. And then he goes wild.

He springs and makes a straight line for we three reluctantly plucky youths, computer parts crunching beneath his feet. "Meat!" he cries. "You're made of meat!"

His eyes fix on mine. "Meat boy! Juicy meat boy!"

"Run, Keegan!" Gloriana screams. "We've got a cannibal situation!"

Wallace's teeth clack like an animated skull, and his twitching fingers reach for my throat. Flecks of saliva fly from his mouth. "Meat!"

There's no escape. The elevator doors have shut, and the furniture provides no hiding place. I'm going to be eaten by a personal assistant in a baby-blue sweater.

My eyes scan Corn's desk for something to throw at

the hungry assistant—a paperweight, a tape dispenser, a stapler. But all Corn's got are a rubber band and a few paper clips. Trying to make do with what's available, I shoot the rubber band at him. It's a good hit, right between the eyes.

"Ow!" Wallace whines. "Bad meat." He lunges for me, fingernails raking my cheek.

"Yes, I'm very bad, I'm rotten meat, I'm eighty-five pounds of food poisoning!"

"Eighty-five pounds of meat!"

"No, no, a lot of that weight is water and bones!"

I cannot believe my last words will be about how much meat I contain.

Wallace is on me, clutching my shirt, and all I can see are incisors and bicuspids.

And then Wallace miraculously rises in the air.

It's Tank.

He's got Wallace around the waist from behind, lifting him off his feet. Wallace thrashes, kicks, twists his neck to try to bite Tank.

Corn giggles. "Brilliant thinking, plucky youths. You've brought a large boy."

"Even more meat!" Wallace gibbers.

Tank leans his head away from Wallace's teeth. "I need to put him down somewhere."

Corn pulls a little clicker device from his pocket. A wall panel opens, revealing a vault with racks of hung jeans and Happy Town T-shirts and running shoes displayed like museum exhibits. "Coat closet," he says.

Tank struggles over to the closet and puts Wallace down with a shove that by Tank's standards is violent. Wallace growls and swipes at him, and Corn clicks the device again. The panel shuts with Wallace inside the closet.

Corn resumes dumping stuff in the acid barrel. "Well, there you go, I saved your lives, you're welcome. Now I need you to take over for Wallace. You can shred documents and gather up the rest of the computer stuff."

"We don't work for you," spits Gloriana.

"Everyone in Happy Town works for me."

"I'd like to resign, please," Tank says.

Wallace pounds the wall with dull thuds. "Let me out! I'm starving! I haven't had a Meat Cramwich in twenty minutes!"

"First question," I begin. "Is the combination of advertising and imps turning the grown-ups of Happy Town into band-instrument-hoarding, excessive-number-of-hat-wearing, Meat-Cramwich-devouring-and-possibly-cannibalistic zombies?"

Corn checks his watch. "Obviously. Though I prefer to

call them consumers. Because they consume things."

"Second question: Why aren't you affected?"

"I don't wear an imp. They're experimental technology and very dangerous."

Gloriana knocks a Happy Town mug off his coffee station. It lands on the soft carpet without breaking.

I'm as disappointed as Gloriana. "New question: Did you do this on purpose?"

Corn sneezes. Maybe he's allergic to battery acid. "The answer to your question is complicated. I *did* intend to create band-instrument-hoarding, excessive-number-of-hat-wearing, Meat-Cramwich-devouring consumers. But the cannibals are a happy accident."

"What's happy about cannibals?"

"I said I didn't mean for that to happen, and I'm telling the truth. Yes, I purchased the implant technology. Yes, I conceived the notion that the imps would make people who wear them susceptible to advertising. Yes, I tested the system in an enclosed habitat where I could control all the conditions and prevent interference from pests who don't share my grand vision. And, yes, the adult residents of Happy Town desire trombones and hats and Meat Cramwiches because I want them to." He checks his watch again. "I hope I satisfied your curiosity, but we're just about out of time, so—"

"But why?" I demand. "Why did you do all this? Just to sell Happy Town junk?"

"You're only children, not the world's number-one galaxy brain, so I'll make this simple. If you can control what people want, you can control what they think. You can control what they do. You can control how they vote in elections. You can make them live in a way that advances society. And above all, you can make them happy, and isn't making people happy the kindest thing you can do?"

"You made my stepdad buy a sousaphone."

"And wasn't he happy?"

I must admit that Carl really was happy with his sousaphone. But I'm not happy. My lungs feel squeezed. Pressure builds in my head. My earlobes are hot. I cannot go with this flow. "You have to turn off the implants and give the grown-ups their brains back."

Corn giggles. "And how do you propose I do that? You think I've got some giant computer with a big red OFF switch?"

"That would have been a good idea," says Tank.

"There's got to be a way to deactivate the imps," I insist.

"Of course there is. But first you'd need to go to med

school and become a doctor with a specialty in brain surgery. In any case, it would be very dangerous. My employees
might start doing horrible things. They might demand better pay and working conditions. They might form a union.
Ick. Any more questions?"

Gloriana points at the acid barrel. "What's up with
that?"

"My computers have evidence proving I knew the risks
of the imps. So, I'm destroying the evidence."

"That makes sense," Gloriana says. "If you're a supervillain."

"I like to think of myself as more of a kaiju. You know,
one of those giant movie monsters?"

"I am familiar with the genre," says Tank. "*Lizards in
Love*. She's an enormous lizard. So is she."

"A kaiju is an exceptional creature," Corn explains, as
if Tank hadn't just spoken. "They're misunderstood and
feared by society because they have the power and willing-
ness to cause change."

"By 'change' do you mean knocking down buildings
and turning cities into flaming wreckage?" Tank says.

I don't know why I ever thought for even a second that
Corn was a genius. It's just a thing people say. *Arlo Corn, he's*

a genius. We should make Arlo Corn the president; he's a genius. Arlo Corn's worth billions of dollars; he must be a genius.

Corn's watch beeps, and a hatch in the ceiling opens like flower petals greeting the sun. The top of the dome looms a few feet above the ceiling, close enough that if you stood on Corn's desk you could tap the glass with a broom stick.

From his desk drawer he takes a pair of goggles and a gray helmet with a pale-green happy face painted on it.

"Are those laser goggles and an internet helmet?" Tank asks.

Corn fastens a chin strap. "Nope, just safety goggles and a regular helmet."

I hate to ask but I have to. "And you need goggles and a helmet why?"

In answer, he clicks his little clicker thingy again. Another hatch whirrs open, this one in the dome itself, and a violent wind blasts through the office, whipping shredded paper bits into a swirling storm. I tuck my face into my shoulder to protect my eyes and can barely hear myself shouting to my friends over the roar of an engine and the distinct whup-whup of rotor blades.

A rope ladder drops through the hatch. Before any of us can stop him, Corn puts a foot on a rung and holds on as the helicopter winches the ladder up. I dive for him, but he's already out of reach.

"Good luck, plucky youths!" Corn calls down as he rises through the hatches. "And don't forget to be happy!"

At least that's what I think he says. The helicopter engine has a punishing roar.

The hatch in the dome and the hatch in the ceiling close, and just like that, Corn has abandoned the disaster he created.

The paper storm settles, but I do not.

"Did that really happen?" says Gloriana. "Did we just watch a full-on supervillain escape like a supervillain in a movie where supervillains escape like that?"

Tank dabs his face with a finger, smearing blood droplets from paper cuts. "Studies show exposure to mass media can negatively influence behavior."

Gloriana wipes a forearm across her own face. "That's why my mom won't let me play *Gut Splatter 4: The Guttening*."

"Aw, too bad, that's a good game. Keegan, you okay?

"Yep."

"You sure?"

"Mm-hmm."

I can only say "yep" and "mm-hmm" because I've been struck speechless by the ridiculously turbulent last five minutes. Coming to see Arlo Corn was my idea. I wasn't sure he'd be helpful, but I did not expect this chapter of our ordeal to go this way.

Meanwhile, Wallace bangs from inside the closet. "Meat!" he wails. "I need meat!"

TWELVE

"We should go home and check on our families." I've recovered my powers of speech, though I'm still discouraged, disgruntled, disgusted, and probably a lot of other "dis" words I don't know.

Tank and Gloriana follow me as I step into the street in front of Corn Tower.

"My mom's not home," Gloriana says. "She'll be working her shift at the Fulfillment Center."

"And I don't want to go home," says Tank. "If I'm going to get devoured, I don't want it to be by my dad. That could complicate our relationship, and not in a fun way."

"We should at least call them." I thumb my phone screen, but there're no bars, no network.

Tank and Gloriana check their phones and report the same.

"I don't know what to do," I whisper, more to myself than to my friends. "We can't call anyone, and even if we could, chances are they'd be consumers like Wallace."

"We'll think of something," Tank assures me. "By the way, I liked how aggressive you were with Corn."

Gloriana agrees. "You were all, 'I want answers, Corn! Spill them or you'll be sorry!'"

"I didn't say any of that. Not in those words."

"It was in your stern expression," Tank says. "It was a good hero moment."

"Oh, please, I'm not a hero."

"How do you know?" Gloriana says. "We can all be heroes in this story. We might have to be."

Adults stumble down the sidewalks and in the streets. They grimace, showing teeth while their eyes dart, desperately looking for something. It's no mystery what they're seeking. A trio of blimps the size of killer whales blast the Meat Cramwich jingle from the sky.

"I don't even know what kind of story this is," I say. "I thought we were in a weird mystery, but it's looking more like a zombie disaster story."

"Then we *really* have to be heroes," Tank declares. "Heroes fight to survive. And they help others survive. They overcome obstacle after obstacle, and they don't give up. And in the end, they win. Usually. And they change their world for the better. Maybe I'll have to make a big stirring speech. Maybe you'll have to take charge and be a leader."

"What about me?" Gloriana asks.

"Sometimes being a hero is just remaining your true self," I say.

"My true self just likes breaking stuff."

I exhale a long sigh. I guess part of going with the flow is continuing to flow even when the waters get choppy, so I recommit myself to flowing.

I am Keegan. I float on the tides like driftwood.

The street grows more crowded with adults streaming from the buildings as if there's a fire drill. After what happened with Wallace, I feel like a halibut at a shark party.

A man in a Happy Town polo shuffles past the conveyor stop. His nostrils flare. He sniffs. Then his head turns with a snap and he locks eyes with me. His tongue lolls, and he rasps, "Meat."

Others change their walking trajectories and head

toward us. "Kid tenders," one of them says, dribbling.

Gloriana's hands search for something to throw. "What do we do?"

"We really could use a plan," Tank says. "They don't look like they're in the mood for stirring speeches."

My legs tell me to run before my brain does. "I think we should get out of here," says my mouth.

"Nothing to fear," says a woman in very crisp business suit. "Everything's going to be okay."

I find her unconvincing, but I'm hopeful. "How is everything okay?"

"I'm an adult," she says in a reassuring tone. "I know things are scary and out of control, and I'm going to help you. I'm going to take you someplace safe BEFORE I SCRAPE THE FLESH OFF YOUR BONES WITH MY TEETH. Oh, wait, I don't know why I said that. I didn't mean—"

"Okay, really, let's run away," I suggest.

"I think we should fight," says Gloriana.

"I don't think that's a good—"

With windmilling fists, Gloriana charges the nearest consumer.

"Gloriana, nooooo!" screams Tank, chasing after her.

I don't feel much like a hero or a leader. More like the

first casualty in a horror movie. But I dutifully chase after Tank and Gloriana to face my destiny.

Consumers swarm Tank and Gloriana, hands reaching for their faces and throats.

"Leave them alone!" I demand in what starts off as an authoritative voice but is ruined by a squeak. What a great time for my voice to start changing.

Heads turn, red-rimmed eyes focusing on me. There's nowhere to hide—not a trash bin, a parked car, or a decent tree in sight. My world is a blur of grasping fingers and wet teeth and whirling voices speaking various sentences that all contain the words "hungry" and "meat."

I've never been in a fight. I've never done wrestling in PE. I haven't even taken an introductory lesson at a shopping-center Tae Kwon Do school. No, I'm not a hero. I'm a chicken nugget. But what I lack in skill and knowledge, I make up for in fear-driven ferocity. I spin like a tornado, throwing wild punches and lashing out unaimed kicks.

Fingernails scratch my cheek. A hand clamps down on my wrist. Teeth. So many teeth.

And then? Then it all stops.

The four or five consumers trying to bite me let go and move away.

"I must be a lethal fighter," I think, catching my breath. "This is good for my self-esteem!"

But a moment later I understand that the consumers aren't running away from me. They're running *toward* the conveyor rolling up the street. The sign above the windshield says, "FULFILLMENT CENTER EXPRESS."

"There'll be meat there," says a consumer.

"Yes, all the meat," says someone else.

"Maybe even Meat Cramwiches, the Microwaveable Meat Sandwiches Crammed with Meat."

The consumers storm the conveyor, leaping on the bumpers, scrambling onto the roof, and the conveyor continues with those who haven't managed to grab on sprinting after it.

My breaths come in gulps, and my heart beats like a hummingbird's.

"Are you two okay?" I wheeze to my friends.

Gloriana scowls in the direction of the conveyor. "I'm okay, but I swear on Arlo Corn's grave I will never again find myself without stuff to hurl and break."

"How about you, Tank?"

"Physically I'm fine. Emotionally I'm a wreck. What should we do? Hide?"

Hiding is exactly what I want. I want to be somewhere safe. Somewhere secure. Maybe a bank vault. Does Happy Town even have a bank? But then what? How long before the cannibalistic adult population of Happy Town runs down every kid? How long before their need for meat becomes competitive? Will they start hurting each other?

This isn't anyone's fault but Corn's. He put everyone in danger, kids and adults alike. Including Carl. Including Mom.

"No," I decide. "We're not going to hide. We're going to get help."

"Nobody in Happy Town's gonna help us," Gloriana says. "We're on our own."

"That's why we're going to get help from the outside."

Gloriana frowns at her phone. "If we can't call home, how are we going to contact the outside?"

"In person," I tell her.

"You mean . . ."

"That's right. We're going to escape Happy Town."

Tank's eyes light up and he pumps his fist. "Yes!"

I appreciate the gesture of confidence.

I'm pretty sure Tank's faking it.

THIRTEEN

Tank and Gloriana keep a watch out for consumers while I try to open the hatch of a MICE hole in the street.

Gloriana's taken off her shoe to use as a weapon, just in case. "My mom used to be a professional fast-pitch softball player, and she taught me how to throw with force and accuracy."

I've never found my mom's job interesting. Thermal duct deployment manager? What even is that? For a while I thought she managed ducks, but then she corrected me and told me her job has something to do with tunnels, which is way less interesting than ducks, obviously.

"The way out of town is by underground train," I announce. "It's fast enough to get us to Las Vegas in half an hour, and once we're there, we'll tell people what's going on in Happy Town and they'll gather the Army and scientists and disaster relief, and hopefully this whole thing will be over soon."

Tank looks grim. "I don't like the idea of leaving my dad behind."

Gloriana looks even more grim. "If my mom's busy chasing meat, I bet she's not taking her meds."

"I don't want to leave my mom and stepdad behind, either. But the best thing we can do for them is get help."

Tank mulls it over. "Then I guess we *choo-choo* away."

"The trains don't go *choo-choo*," Gloriana says. "They go *zhroooom*."

Tank frowns. "I'd say it's more like a *whooooom*."

"That's not even close. Maybe *swoooooooosh*."

"*Hogga hogga wommm wommmm*."

"Nothing goes *hogga hogga*, Tank."

"I guess you're right. How about *badoosh caroom*?"

"If you two are done making train noises, maybe we could figure out how to open the portal."

Gloriana puts her shoe back on. "Like this." She raises her knee and brings her foot down in a powerful stomp. The portal hatch whirrs and opens, revealing steel ladder rungs descending into darkness.

"Where'd you learn to do that?" asks Tank, delighted.

"I stomp on a lot of stuff just to see what happens."

Lucky Gloriana's on my side. I start down the ladder.

It's a long way down, eventually ending in a concrete tunnel with a ceiling so low we have to hunch to avoid scraping our heads. Sporadic utility lights cast a weak orange glow.

I peer into the dim distance. "This way, I think."

Every few hundred yards we come across a MICE burdened with cardboard boxes, dead in its tracks. I give one a cautious kick with my toe. "What do you think killed them?"

Gloriana gives it a harder kick. "With the adults transformed into meat-craving zombies, it's not surprising the city's systems are shutting down. Automated stuff still needs people to keep it running. That's probably why there's no phone signal."

"Could we move on, please?" Tank says. "Dead robots make dark tunnels even more creepy."

At that exact moment, the unmistakable sound of footsteps echoes down the tunnel.

Gloriana takes her shoe off again.

I do the same, even though I'm bad at throwing.

Tank takes his off, too. I have no idea whether he can throw or not, but at least his shoe is very large.

A familiar voice sounds out: "Keegan? Keegan, is that you?"

My breath catches.

"The consumer knows you," Gloriana whispers. "That's so much creepier than a consumer stranger."

A figure emerges from the shadows.

Her shirt is half-untucked, the pocket torn and dangling by a few threads like loose skin.

"Mom?"

"Oh! Keegan!" She rushes forward and hugs me in what is probably the best mom hug of all time.

"Are you okay, Mom? What are you doing here?"

"I'm a thermal duct deployment manager. This is a thermal duct. The better question is what are you doing here . . . ?" She notices my friends for the first time.

"This is Tank and Gloriana. Tank and Gloriana, this is my mom."

"Hi, Keegan's mom, it's nice to meet you," Tank says in the tone one might use to say "Who's a good puppy?" to a viciously snarling dog.

"You're all banged up, Mom. You sure you're okay?"

"I'm really fine, sweetie! I just got in a fight with some of my coworkers."

"Over what?" Gloriana asks. She kneels on one knee to untie her other shoe.

Mom bites her lower lip. "Meat," she says in a small voice as her stomach audibly rumbles. She attempts a reassuring smile but only manages a caricature of one. She digs her fingernails into her palms.

"Oh, Mom, no."

"I'm sorry, sweetie. I'm trying not to, but I don't think I can keep it up. It's almost like there's a voice in my head telling me to do hideous things, and no matter how much I yell at it, it just keeps getting louder."

I shake my head. "I know you, Mom. You're the strongest person I've ever met. You can fight it."

Tears stream down her cheeks. "You'll have to be stronger, Keegan. All of you. Because we're not strong enough."

Gloriana grips her shoe and cocks back her throwing arm while Tank places a hand on my shoulder. "C'mon, Keegan, we should go."

"I'm not leaving my mom like this. Mom, we're leaving the city. And you're coming with us."

"No, your friend's right, honey. Please go. I don't want to hurt you." The shaking in her voice wounds me deeper than any bite.

"If you won't come with us, then I'm staying. Tank and

Gloriana, you have to get out. I'll give you both my shoes."

Mom gives me a smile that breaks my heart. "I love you, Keegan," she says, lunging for me. I jerk back, barely avoiding her gnashing teeth.

Gloriana chucks her shoe and strikes my mom square in the face.

"Don't hit my mom!"

Mom growls and comes at me again, saliva dripping from the corners of her mouth.

Tank clamps a hand around my arm and wrenches me away. Mom makes another lunge and gets Gloriana's other shoe in her face.

"Keegan, we have to go!" Tank says desperately, dragging me.

"I know," I say, my vision blurry with tears. "I know."

We race down the tunnel with Mom's rapid footsteps behind us.

"Hurry," Mom shouts. "I'm a good runner and I don't want to catch you! Get word to the outside. Tell them, Keegan, tell them!"

The sound of her footfalls grows distant, and after a while, so does her voice. The last thing I hear her scream is, "RUN! I'M SO HUNGRY!"

FOURTEEN

Sweating and heaving, we follow the tunnel until it ends at the train hangar, a great dark cavern of concrete and steel and bare rock with a vaulted ceiling so high it's lost in shadow. Every footfall on the smooth concrete floor resounds like a hammer blow. Every breath is a gruff expulsion.

The locomotive, silent on a single track, looks like something from the future, a sleek rocket linked to a line of cars longer than three soccer fields. Its rounded nose cone aims at a pair of massive steel doors about a hundred yards away, shut as though the train is a caged beast.

"Here's our way out," I say, trying to keep shame out of my voice. My own mother tried to bite my face off, yet the idea of leaving her behind feels like a betrayal.

"It's either our way out or the death of us," Gloriana says.

"Why?" Tank cries, exasperated. "Why did you say that?"

"Were any of your romance books been about escaping zombies on a train?"

"As a matter of fact—"

"Was the train packed with zombies?"

"No," Tank answers with a tinge of defiance. "It was packed with puppies."

"Zombie puppies?"

Tank looks scandalized. "Of course not. The puppies helped teach the zombies the meaning of love."

"All I'm saying is be careful. The train is automated, so hopefully there's nobody down here except us. But maybe the cargo cars are packed with lunch meat and inevitable consumers."

I give the locomotive door a tug. It opens with a wincingly loud clank. A short set of stairs leads up inside the cab. There are seats and a wide dashboard crowded with various controls and gauges. "If it's automated, why's there a crew compartment?"

"Corn probably just bought a standard locomotive and

had it modified," Gloriana says. "Buying stuff seems to be the one thing he's good at."

If we can get the train beyond the hangar doors, we'll find open desert and eventually Las Vegas.

But first we have to figure out how to make this thing go.

"Did you know the first roller coasters were just super hazardous mining trains?" Tank says. "I learned that from *Love Is a Roller Coaster*."

"Did it tell you how to operate a train?" asks Gloriana.

"In fact it did. If only this was a one-hundred-and-fifty-year-old steam train . . ."

Tank finds a clipboard hanging from a hook and starts flipping through loose paper pages. "This is a cargo manifest. Let's see . . . diapers, diapers, more diapers . . . I had no idea there were so many kinds of diapers. I'm going to skip past the diapers. Here we go. Jigsaw puzzles. Leaf blowers. Laundry pods. Cat food. Canned tuna. Beef jerky. Liverwurst pâté. Those little sausages they serve on toothpicks at fancy parties . . ."

"Great," says Gloriana. "What could possibly go wrong."

Tank flips up the last page on the clipboard and finds a

laminated card. "Oh, here we go, it's a user guide. Do you see a big green button that says GO?"

I scan over the puzzle of controls and find a button that is, indeed, big and green and is labeled GO.

"Got it." I crack my knuckles, take a breath, and press the button. The control panel hums to life with glowing screens. A moment later, a deep vibration thrums beneath my feet. The beast is waking up.

Tank gives me a thumbs-up and reads off the user guide. "Move the throttle forward. That's the lever over on your left. Hangar doors will open when the proximity sensors detect the train at optimal distance. Doors will reseal when the train has cleared the hangar."

That's good. Because the last thing we want to do is take off at full speed and smash into solid steel doors like an overripe peach.

I wrap my fingers around the throttle and push it just the tiniest bit forward.

The train thunders off like a rocket.

And the hangar doors do not open.

And the train smashes into them, exactly like an overripe peach.

We stagger from the locomotive and take in the scene. Knocked off the rail, the locomotive lies on its side like roadkill in a field of crumpled steel. The cargo cars, crumpled like an accordion bellows, creak and moan in a haze of smoke and a jumble of diapers and meat products. The hangar doors aren't even scratched.

"Ow," I whine.

"Ow," Tank agrees, coughing.

"Lots and lots of ow," Gloriana contributes, spitting out a glass pebble.

"We're all somehow alive." I rub my aching head. "How is that even possible?"

"I don't remember much," Gloriana says, probing her mouth with her tongue for more glass. "There was all this noise and then I went flying, but something big and soft broke my fall."

Tank raises a hand. "That was me. I broke my fall on the hard control panel."

"I didn't break my fall," I say. "I just got broken."

Tank starts checking me over with the gentleness of a parent and the thoroughness of a surgeon. "Where does it hurt?"

"Everywhere. But all my moving parts seem to be

working. What about you, Gloriana?"

She doesn't answer.

"Gloriana?"

"Oh? Sorry, I'm fine." She gestures at the ruins of the train. "It's just as a fan of breaking things, I'm having a happy moment."

"You're very weird," I inform her.

"I know." She spits another piece of glass.

Rotating a sore shoulder, I survey the wreckage. "I guess we're all basically okay. We should get out of here before consumers—"

A voice rings out: "Hello, there!" A tweedy man enters the hangar from one of the tunnels. "Looks like you've got some meat."

I swear if I survive this day I will never eat meat again. Heck, I won't eat another living thing. I shall become a plastictarian.

"All kinds of good meat here," I say, thinking fast. "Liver pâté! Tiny sausages! Help yourself!"

"Much better than stringy kid meat," says Gloriana.

"Never been much of a pâté fan, to tell you the truth."

The tweedy man isn't alone. Half a dozen more consumers trail behind him.

"But pâté is good," insists Tank. "You can spread it on stuff."

"You can spread anything if you smoosh it enough," the tweedy man argues quite reasonably. "Anyway, it'll still be there after I've picked your bones clean."

"Maybe you'll end up liking pâté," Tank says, still trying to win him over.

"Could be!"

More and more consumers gather in the hangar, enough to fill a bus, then enough to fill a classroom, all approaching with slow inevitability. Murmurs fill the cavernous space. It's hard to make out individual words in the rising flood of voices, but "meat" and "hunger" and "bite" and "tasty" stick out. The crowd inches closer and closer to us, and we back up until we're pressed against the wreckage.

"I still think I can convince them that pâté is a superior form of meat," Tank says.

Gloriana made a blah face. "No way, liver is super gross, and it's even worse when you mash it into a paste."

The consumers are so close I can make out the arteries in their bloodshot eyes. I draw a big breath. It hurts my bruised ribs, but I hold it another moment before hollering as loud as I can. "MEAT CRAMWICHES!!! THERE'S

MEAT CRAMWICHES IN THE WRECKAGE!!"

"Meat Cramwiches are delicious," Tank says.

Gloriana makes a face. "Not really."

Thankfully, the consumers are more enthusiastic about Meat Cramwiches than they are about us. They slowly turn to the derailed box cars. One of them finds a mangled cardboard box, gasps, and grabs a handful of plastic bags. He rips them open and stuffs no fewer than nine jerky strips into his mouth. After that, the consumers go into full-on riot mode. There's screaming. There's pushing. There's scratching and kicking. And there is even a great deal of liver pâté consumption.

Tank and I make a move to dash for the tunnels, but Gloriana lingers. She seems dazed.

"What's wrong? We have to go before they eat everything and find out I was lying about Meat Cramwiches."

Gloriana shakes her head as if coming out of a trance. "Oh, right. Sorry. You know me and broken things." She gestures at the swarming mob of consumers. "This is the most broken thing I ever saw."

FIFTEEN

We poke our heads out a MICE hole like wary gophers and emerge in an alley behind a theater. The pavement glitters with broken glass. A garbage trolley lies on its side with its garbage guts spilling out. If consumers already picked over the alley in a meat hunt, maybe they won't be back.

"There," Gloriana says, looking toward the end of the alley. Consumers stumble past the alley's mouth.

I point at the theater's back door and whisper, "Hide."

There's a delivery portal at the foot of the door the size of a large pet flap.

"Think you can get through that?" I ask Tank.

"Maybe. They sell popcorn at the snack bar, so if I get

stuck you can grease me up with fake butter."

We scurry from the MICE hole to the portal and all three of us get through, even Tank, without needing fake butter lubricant.

The green tinge from a flickering fluorescent light reveals a storage room with artificial foliage and a costume wardrobe. Plywood boards painted with scenes of deserts and forests and castles lean against the walls. I'd assumed this was a movie theater, but it looks more like they do plays here, which means the black curtain along the far wall probably leads to a stage.

Tank drags a table over to barricade the portal, and I distribute flashlights from a toolbox to my friends.

"Anything I can throw?" Gloriana asks, eyes gleaming with hope.

"What's your weapon of choice? Screwdriver? Tape measure? Hammer?"

"Ooh, hammer, please. And we should check out the rest of the theater in case there's a writhing nest of consumers drawn by the smell of overpriced hot dogs."

"Whee," I say.

It is a sarcastic "whee."

Flashlights in hand (and in Gloriana's case, a giant claw

hammer as well) we peek through the curtain and peer out into the seats.

"Awesome," says Gloriana. "There's only a million places for consumers to hide in the dark."

"We all stay together," Tank says. "None of this splitting-up nonsense they do in horror movies."

In a creeping huddle, we shine our flashlights between the rows. I'm almost surprised we don't find a crouching consumer picking morsels off a human thigh bone. But there's still the lobby to check.

Consumers have hit the place hard. The front door's been forced open, and people have ransacked the snack bar. The popper is full of yellow popcorn, and the candy counter is still stocked, but the clear cover over the hot dog warmer's been wrenched off its hinges. There aren't any hot dogs left inside, just metal rollers glistening with residue grease.

I read the menu board to see if there're any other meat products for sale. "Looks like they nabbed the Happy Tenders and Happy Weenies and ran."

Tank drags a lobby sofa over and leans it against the broken door. "This'll slow anyone down who tries to get in, and the noise will give us a heads-up."

"I guess we can hide here for a while. Or even a long

time. We'll sustain ourselves with candy and popcorn and soda and Slurry." I like my plan. We'll just hunker down until someone else conveniently solves the consumer problem. The thought of setting our burden aside so someone else can fix things lightens my shoulders.

We stuff chocolate bars in our pockets and fill up bucket-sized soda cups before heading back into the auditorium.

When I part the curtain between the stage and backstage I have to bite the insides of my cheeks to keep from screaming. A grinning skull stares me in the face.

Hot pins and needles ignite my muscles, telling my legs to move, but fear freezes me in place. I drop my cup. Cold bubbly soda pop soaks into my socks.

After an instant, I realize the skull belongs to a marionette hanging in an open cupboard alongside a clown, a monkey, a pirate, a king, and dozens of other puppets suspended from hooks.

"You okay?"

It's Tank's comforting voice.

"Nope. I wasn't expecting puppets."

"That's my fault. I should have warned you. This is a puppet theater."

"Puppets? Why puppets?"

"Corn loves puppets. So going to puppet shows is a good career move."

I slump against a scenic backdrop of a giant beanstalk. "We're all Corn's puppets. He plotted this whole disaster. He wrote the script. We're tangled up in his strings, and I bet he's relaxing in his private jet, eating diamonds and laughing."

I shut my eyes because I no longer want to see things—not the puppets, not anything related to Happy Town, not any part of the world.

No, I am not okay. There're all the consumers outside to deal with. And I've crashed a train. I've abandoned Mom in the tunnels to fight over meat with other consumers. I should have done something to help her. I should have stayed with her no matter what.

"You know those obstacles you mentioned, Tank? How many of them do you have to overcome until you're a hero?"

Tank is quiet for a while, thinking. "I don't think it really works like that. There's this science fiction romance series I like—*Star Crossed*. It's about these people falling in love who band together to defeat the tyrannical Extreme Leader and his Shadow Empire. By the end of the third book, they beat the tyrant and free the galaxy and get married. Then the second trilogy starts twenty years later and, guess what, now an even more powerful and more evil regime has risen."

"Do the good guys win?"

"For a while."

"But the bad guys come back again?"

"I hope so, because that means more books. But I guess my point is—"

"There's always going to be obstacles. You never stop fighting. You never get to be the hero."

"You've almost got it," Tank said. "The thing is, you might have to do heroic things, but you don't have to be the only one."

Gloriana gives me a light punch on the arm. "And the good news is I'm already a hero as long as I have things to throw." She wiggles her hammer.

I laugh history's tiniest laugh. "I hate Happy Town, but if I'd never come here, I never would have met you two."

"So, I guess it's worth it," says Tank.

"Let's not go overboard."

Then, a noise.

Not loud. Just something like the scrape of a mouse behind a wall.

"What was that?" Tank mouths.

Gloriana points to the puppet cupboard. She mouths,

"It came from behind the puppets."

I shrug to communicate "What should we do now?"

Tank returns the shrug to say he doesn't know. Or else he's signaling that he doesn't know what my shrug meant.

I shrug again, this time more elaborately.

Tank returns with a yet-more-elaborate shrug, and Gloriana mimes choking someone, by which she probably means she wants to choke someone.

A second noise.

Gloriana aims her hammer at the puppet cupboard.

Tank picks up a metal folding chair.

My eyes dart about for a weapon of my own. I don't find anything, so I arm myself with the chocolate-and-nougat bar I stole from the concessions stand. It feels pretty hard. Maybe I could sharpen it into a nougat knife.

Gloriana raises her hammer to bring down thunder and pain. Tank lifts the folding chair above his head. I wield my candy bar.

With a grim nod, I put my hand on the monkey puppet and mouth a count.

"One."

Maybe there's nobody here. Maybe the sound we heard was just settling pipes. Maybe it was just a mouse.

"Two."

And maybe this is all a dream and I'm going to wake up safe in bed.

"Three."

I sweep the hanging puppets aside.

A man sits on the cupboard floor, eyes wide with fear and ferocity like a raccoon cornered in an attic. We've caught him in the act of transferring a chicken nugget from a paper tray into his already stuffed mouth.

His bottom lip is swollen. Bloody scratches crisscross his cheeks. His fingernails are broken. Me and my friends have been struggling to survive a zombie plague, but the consumers are combatants in a meat war. They're even worse off than we are.

I motion for Tank and Gloriana to lower their weapons.

"Sir?" I begin. "We're sorry we broke into your hiding place."

The consumer chews.

"You don't have to worry about your nuggets. None of us wants your nuggets. You don't have to be afraid. Nobody wants to hurt you."

"So now I'm nobody?" mutters Gloriana.

"Everyone's just trying to stay alive," I go on. "So, it

would be great if you promised not to eat us, and then we could join forces and put an end to—"

The consumer clutches the remaining nuggets in a white-knuckled grip. "Mine, mine, mine!" he cackles.

"Yes, yours. Nobody's trying to take them away."

"MINE!"

He springs, colliding into me and knocking me to the floor. Ragged fingernails claw my face. A knee to the gut punches the air from my lungs. A blur of limbs. Gasping breath. Everyone screaming. A sharp pain in my forearm.

"GET OFF HIM!" screams Tank. He and Gloriana pry the consumer away and give him a powerful shove into a potted plastic tree. He bares his teeth, still cradling his nuggets. Tank retrieves the folding chair and carries it like a shield. Gloriana grips her hammer.

Scrambling to my feet, I display my open palms. "Just calm down," I say, trying to catch my breath. "You are more than your fears and appetites. You are a human being. You have a brain. Try to focus on who you were before you got your imp."

"MINE!" With a gargling scream, the consumer bolts out the back door.

"Good riddance," Gloriana says, still clutching her hammer.

Wincing, I feel my scratched-up face. "That was probably the most sucky few seconds of my life. We should reinforce the barricade and—"

"Keegan," Tank says, almost inaudibly, his face bright with alarm. "Your arm."

I look down at the meaty part of my left forearm. A ring of tooth indentations marks a sloppy wound, the flesh torn and bleeding. And now that I'm aware of it, the full brunt of pain arrives, aching, stinging, burning, all at the same time.

With the pain comes a dawning horror. I've been bitten by a zombie.

SIXTEEN

"We need to soak your bite in battery acid," Gloriana declares. "There was a whole barrel of it in Corn's office."

"I am not soaking my arm in battery acid."

"You got bit by a zombie, Keegan. That means you're infected. You're my friend, and I don't want to see you become a zombie, so we have to burn the zombie cooties."

"That's not how this zombie plague works." Tank tears the clown puppet's costume, rips it up, and ties a strip of fabric around my forearm.

"How many zombie plagues have you been through?" Gloriana counters. "We don't know how this one works. Keegan, do you want to eat a Meat Cramwich? Do you want to eat human flesh?"

I close my eyes against the pain. My blood's already soaking through the clown clothes. "I'd rather eat a shoe. "

Gloriana narrows her eyes in suspicion. "Now you want to eat shoes?"

"Nobody's dipping anything in acid," says Tank. "But we need to get Keegan to a hospital. It's a bad bite, and there's probably a whole jacuzzi of mouth germs in there, consumer or not. The hospital's four blocks away. If we're lucky we can make it."

I snort. "If we're lucky the hospital won't be full of consumers having a food fight."

"I choose to ignore your negativity. Gloriana, what do you want to do?"

She hesitates a few seconds before giving in. "If the consumer who bit Keegan tells other consumers about us, they could bust in and overwhelm us, so we need to get out of here. We might as well try the hospital."

"Can you run?" Tank asks.

"I don't need my arm to run."

As Tank and Gloriana peek out the delivery portal to check the route for danger, I spot a dirty rubber eraser on the floor.

No, not an eraser.

It's a chicken nugget.

It gives me a thought.

I slip the nugget into my pocket.

The Arlo Corn Philanthropic Hospital is a sixteen-story white box that could have come from an ice cube tray. At least it's not an old creepy hospital. Instead, it's a new creepy hospital. The electricity has failed, either due to consumers neglecting the power grid or because everything in Happy Town is broken and nothing works.

It's not even really a hospital yet. There're few walls, mostly just steel framing and an open ceiling revealing cables and wires and conduit. Two-by-fours lie across sawhorses amid piles of other construction materials and tools.

We probe the darkness with our flashlights. "They haven't made any progress on this place since the last time I was here," says Gloriana, inspecting a circular saw.

"You come here often?" I ask.

"With all the breaking of stuff I do, I get banged up and cut a lot. Medical supplies are this way. Follow me."

She leads us through more construction areas separated with floor-to-ceiling plastic sheets. The sheets are ragged, half torn down, wavering milky ghosts. I aim my flashlight beam at the ground, not wanting to tip off any hiding consumers.

Gloriana treads lightly in her socks, but every step Tank and I take on the bare concrete floor sounds like a hammer strike.

When we arrive at an exam room, Tank raids the cabinets, and I hop onto the exam table. "You know first aid?"

"With all the books I read about dashing doctors and EMTs and ski rescue medics? Yes. Besides, we're not doing anything fancy here. Rest your elbow on your leg and hold your arm out, please."

Tank gets to work, untying my makeshift clown bandage. A fresh throb of pain makes my eyes water. With alcohol pads, butterfly bandages, and gauze, Tank works to clean and dress the bite.

I contribute by hissing in pain and adding some curse words.

"Thanks," I say when the ordeal is over. "You're good at zombie plague emergency medicine."

"And you're a good but foul-mouthed patient. Now what do we do from here? Risk going back outside, or risk getting trapped inside?"

Gloriana raises her hand. "I vote we stay here. More weapons."

"You know a power saw isn't going to do you much good without power."

"I can tell you've never frisbeed a saw blade."

Tank examines my dressing and adds some more tape. "What's your vote, Keegan?"

"My ideas haven't been working out. You two decide."

"You're at a low point in your journey, Keegan, the dark night of the soul. Which is good news since it's a necessary step on your way to becoming a hero."

I don't know about the hero part, but I'm definitely at a low point.

If someone bites my mom . . .

Or if she eats some kid . . .

"Why aren't you having a dark night of the soul?"

"Oh, I am," Tank says. "It's just that the darkness has a hard time breaking through my sunny disposition."

"What about you, Gloriana?"

"I kick at the darkness until it bleeds daylight."

The pain of my bite wound fades a little. "I haven't known you two very long, but I'm very glad I fell in with you."

"Us too," Gloriana says. "You're the friend we needed to complete our pyramid of friend power. We've tried a few others, but they all burned out after a few days."

Tank and Gloriana can both be pretty intense, but maybe that's a good thing during a zombie disaster.

"I don't know about you guys, but I'm running out of steam," Gloriana says. "We need to rest, and we're not going to be able to do that out in the streets. Let's go down to the morgue and hide in the drawers where they store the bodies. They should be empty. Nobody's died in Happy Town."

"That we know of," says Tank.

"Even if anyone has, who's around to process corpses?"

The route to the morgue goes through more unlit construction areas, past more plastic sheets, down four flights of stairs followed by hallways with so many turns I get a little motion sick, and finally up to a pair of swinging doors.

Tank and Gloriana argue over who will go in first (they both want to), and in the end all three of us press shoulder to shoulder and squeeze in together.

Which turns out to be a massive mistake.

A nest of consumers squats on the floor in circle formation. They're in awful shape, with torn clothes, missing clumps of hair, nasty cuts—all signs of fighting over meat. But they're too busy to fight now.

They're eating.

They grunt and work their jaws with wet chewing sounds. They smack their gums. They grunt. Occasionally someone snaps a bone from their meal, the sound of a firecracker.

It's chicken, I think. There aren't any bodies here. Please be chicken.

I don't breathe, because if I do it's going to come out as a scream.

With aching slowness, we back up and begin closing the door.

Almost casually, one of the consumers turns their head. I focus on their face because I don't want to look at the morsel of meat in their hand.

"Please be chicken," I mouth, almost a prayer.

The consumer shoots to their feet and points. "Fresh kid."

We don't wait for the other consumers to turn. We simply run as though we're on fire.

With Gloriana in the lead, I can only hope she doesn't take us to a dead end where the morgue nest can catch up with us. I wish I'd collected some saw blades to chuck.

Gloriana brings us to a door marked "Authorized Personnel Only."

"I hereby declare us authorized," she says, pushing through the door.

Hunkering, we remain quiet and listen to running footsteps on the other side of the door. When we no longer hear them, I draw a careful breath.

Dank, warm air makes the place feel like an aquarium shop and brings sweat to my armpits. I should have used more Sniffree.

There's electricity here, at least enough to power the red-lensed emergency lights and cast the chamber in a blood-colored monotone. Thick ceramic tiles line the walls and floors, except for a drain in the center of the room. I don't want to think about what gets hosed down here.

"What is this place?" asks Tank.

"I don't know," Gloriana says. "I haven't explored this part of the hospital."

Tank examines a fuse box mounted beside the door. "You know, I think I might be able to rig up an electrified tripwire with this. It won't deliver a strong shock, but if a consumer tries to come in, maybe it'll be enough to discourage them." He starts pulling wires loose from the box. "Before you ask, I learned this from *Tingling Love*. He's a cat burglar. She's an electrician."

"You are amazing," I tell him.

He beams.

Steel racks contain rows of shiny tanks, each equipped with a pancake-sized window glowing blue light. Stenciled letters on the sides of the tanks spell out "CRYBRO."

I step up to one of them, bringing my face close to look inside.

"Oh . . . oh, no. No. This is too much. Just, no."

"I wanna see!" Gloriana shoves me aside and peers in. "Cooool," she croons.

It's a severed head. Bald. Marshmallow-colored flesh coated in a thin frost. Eyes not quite shut.

Gloriana darts from tank to tank. "Yep, all heads."

I do not know what to say about this. School has not prepared me for such occasions. This is an awful flow to go with.

"Should we hide somewhere else?" Tank asks.

I'm willing to hide anywhere else. I am willing to go back to the morgue and hide in an incinerator.

But no. "Better the chamber of horrors with severed

heads in tanks we know than other unspeakable atrocities we don't know. And at least the heads aren't trying to eat us."

Tank goes back to the fuse box to complete his electrical project. "Please don't fail us, romance novel electrician."

Thwap. Thwap. Thwap.

"What was that?" I look inside the tank again in case the severed head has started making *thwap* sounds. The head just stares back.

Gloriana is happy for an excuse to look at heads again, but the *thwaps* are coming from outside the room.

"Footsteps," Tank whispers. "Someone's coming." Oddly, he's wearing a bright smile.

"Why do you look happy about this?"

"I kind of want to see if my tripwire works."

Thwap. Thwap.

Gloriana tries to lift a tank off its shelf, but it's bolted down. "If it doesn't work we can throw the heads."

The footfalls grow heavy. Whatever's coming has big feet.

The *thwaps* pause.

Gloriana clutches her hammer.

Tank curls his fingers into fists.

I adopt some kind of Tae Kwon Do stance even though I still don't know any Tae Kwon Do.

The door creaks open and there stands a young man with big, watery eyes. A sheen of sweat coats his face. Long, lank hair frames his black-and-blue swollen jaw. Maybe he got punched in a meat riot.

He parts his lips and runs his tongue over his teeth with a growl.

Tank's wire stretches across his path, about half an inch above the floor. The consumer can easily look down and avoid stepping across it, so I decide to divert his attention elsewhere.

I do a little dance.

"Hey, over here, look at me! That's right, I'm doing a little dance!" I rub my tummy. "Juicy, juicy, dance, dance!"

Tank enjoys the dance. "Go, Keegan!"

Gloriana does not enjoy the dance. She redoubles her efforts to pry a tank from the shelf.

The consumer drools.

"Juicy, juicy? See me dancing?"

"You're not a good dancer," the consumer says. "But you are made of meat, so . . ."

He steps forward. His ankle crosses the tripwire.

There's an electrical pop, and the consumer yowls. Now he's the one dancing, doing little hops of pain and glaring accusingly at me.

"Don't blame him," Tank says. "That was my fault."

"And there's a lot worse coming if you take another step," I lie.

There's really nothing else coming if he takes another step.

The consumer wipes dribble off his chin and makes a mean face. "That was a lousy thing to do. What are you, vandals?"

"Call us whatever you want," I say. "But we're not going to be your lunch."

"That's fine by me. I'm not even hungry anymore." His expression changes, as if he's just realized something. "Hey, I'm not hungry. How about that!"

I exchange looks with Tank and Gloriana. "Are you saying you don't want to eat us?"

"Oof, no way. I already had a Porksicle, the Nutritious Lickable Porkchop. And half a Meat Cramwich, the Micro—"

"—waveable Meat Sandwich Crammed with Meat," the three of us drone.

"Yeah, and, oh, some fingers. Chicken fingers. Probably. But that nasty shock made me lose my appetite."

"Who are you and what are you doing here?" I demand, still wary.

"I'm Tommy, and I work here. Also, when I still had the craving I thought I'd come down and eat the heads. Heads are really just complicated meatballs when you think about it."

Tommy steps deeper into the chamber and inspects the tanks, checking connections, peering into the windows.

"You kids shouldn't be here. This isn't a playground. You are in the presence of Arlo Corn's most brilliant side project: CRYBRO."

He strikes a pose as if unveiling a magnificent work of art and awaiting applause. When we fail to deliver, he keeps talking. "'Cry' because we provide cryogenic services."

"'Cryogenic,'" repeats Gloriana. "That means freezing stuff."

"I am no closer to understanding what this is all for," I complain.

"What's the 'BRO' part mean?" asks Tank.

"It's short for 'brothers,' because Arlo Corn believes all people are brothers."

Gloriana scowls. "What about sisters?"

"Why, then it'd be CRYSIS. That sounds too much like 'crisis.'"

I let out a long, slow breath, hoping to exhale the hot cloud of impatience building inside. "WHY DOES ARLO CORN HAVE AN UNDERGROUND CHAMBER FULL OF FROZEN HEADS?"

"Because he's a genius. See, people like you and me, we're little people. But Arlo Corn is a big man. Our minds are stuck on today, but not Arlo Corn's. He imagines the future he wants to see, and then he makes that future happen. And I'm not talking about tomorrow. I'm not talking about next week, or the next century. That's little-man thinking. But Arlo Corn, he's a long-termer. He's looking thousands and thousands of years down the road. Tens of thousands. Hundreds of thousands. What's happening now doesn't matter to him any more than the wavering flame of a match matters to a volcano. You see? To understand what he's doing, you have to think like him. But you can't! Because you're not Arlo Corn. You don't have his number-one galaxy brain."

"I think I get it," I say. "People die and they get their heads sawed off and preserved at CRYBRO because they think in the future, we'll be able to cure whatever killed them—old age, disease—and in the future we can probably grow them a new body and plop their brains inside with their memories intact. They pay for this of course. A lot. Right, Tommy?"

He laughs a scornful laugh. "No, what a preposterous . . . Oh, wait. That's actually it, exactly."

Tank gasps. "Keegan! I didn't know you had a galaxy brain!"

"I don't. I just thought of the goofiest reason to keep frozen heads I could come up with. I am sad but not surprised I was right."

Tommy takes umbrage. "Please don't presume to put yourself on the same level as Mr. Arlo Corn. He's a great big man. Sometimes you'll say hello to him and he'll just walk right by and he won't even notice you because he's thinking galaxy-sized thoughts. One time I slipped on a wet floor and fell and cracked my head right in front of him, and he didn't even stop to ask me if I was okay. Because he doesn't concern himself with little-man problems, you see. He's a great man. He's—"

"Maybe if we zap him again, he'll shut up," suggests Gloriana.

"Sorry to interrupt," Tank says, "but is your implant still working?"

Tommy cocks his head to the side and tries to air-type. "Nope. Nothing. You kids broke my implant. You're going to have to pay for that. Now if you'll please leave me and my heads alone . . ."

Gloriana scoffs. "With all those consumers out there? We're staying."

"Actually, no," I announce. "We have to go back outside."

"But why?"

"Because I finally know how we're going to put an end to the consumers."

SEVENTEEN

Late-afternoon sunlight bleeds through the dome and casts Happy Town in a nuclear-orange tint. A food wrapper lies in the middle of the street, still as a dead bird. All is quiet, no consumers in sight. Here and there, I spot a lone shoe, a torn and bloody T-shirt, a necklace, a comb, evidence of a meat riot.

I watch for anything that could be Mom's, because she could have been in the middle of all this violence.

The thought gives me a stomachache.

But I have a plan, and I relay it to Tank and Gloriana as they follow me down the street in the direction of the Fulfillment Center. "Tank's tripwire turned Tommy the CRYBRO back to normal, right?"

"He keeps heads in tanks," Gloriana points out. "That's

pretty far from normal."

"But he didn't want to eat us once he got shocked. So maybe he's not normal, but he's not a consumer anymore."

"Keegan's onto something," says Tank. "The shock must have fried his imp."

"Exactly."

"I don't think I can rig up thousands of tripwires and convince consumers to trip over them."

"You don't have to. We're going to use a different kind of shock-delivering device. One we've got tons of in the Fulfillment Center: Automals."

"That's brilliant, Keegan!" Tank exclaims. "You have chosen to be brilliant!"

Gloriana is less enthusiastic. "The Fulfillment Center's more than two miles away. That's a lot of territory to cross on foot without getting chased down and devoured like water buffalo in a piranha tank."

"It'll take luck," I admit. "And I don't believe in luck. But I'm choosing to be the kind of person who believes in his friends, and who wants his friends to believe in him."

"Inspiring." Gloriana remains unconvinced.

"Everything else we've tried has failed," says Tank. "I figure we're due a win."

"Also, I don't have any other ideas," I add. "So, unless

you've got another plan . . ."

"We've got a plan," says someone.

All three of us yell in unison.

A teenage girl in a black Anarchy Now T-shirt emerges from the shadowed entrance of a boarded-up storefront.

I recover my calm. "Oh, we know you from the Corn Tower. You're a plucky youth."

"Yup, I survived. So did my friends. What's with the bandage on your arm? Did you get bit?"

"He fell on a cactus," Tank says at the exact same time Gloriana says, "He was playing with power tools."

Anarchy Now rolls her eyes.

"I got bit," I confess.

"Me too." She raises her pant leg. "My geometry teacher took a chunk out of my calf. Fortunately, I ran into help and they patched me up."

Her bandage isn't nearly as neatly applied as mine.

Gloriana eyes her wound with suspicion. "Who helped you?"

"The Feral Gang. They took me and my friends in, and they've got a plan to deal with the zombies."

"Corn calls them consumers," I say.

"He can call them whatever he wants, and once we deal with the zombies, we're going to deal with him."

"He got away." Tank twirls his finger in the air and goes, "Whup, whup, whup."

"Figures. Escaping consequences is a rich-guy superpower. Anyway, it's not safe out here. Come inside."

Anarchy Now raps a rhythmic knock on the door. It opens a crack, revealing the face of Nose Ring.

"New recruits?" Nose Ring asks.

"Yep. And they're still alive, so you know they're tough."

I like being called "tough," especially after all the screaming and running away I've done today. Maybe my dark night of the soul is over.

Nose Ring steps aside to let us in and shuts the door after us. Their third friend, Pink Pajamas, gives us a bored "Hey," but when he sees Gloriana's hammer, he nods with approval. He has his own hammer, and Gloriana returns the nod.

I scan the room, engaging in my new habit of looking for consumers whenever I'm in a new place. The windows are boarded up with wood planks, maybe borrowed from the hospital. A steel desk blocks the door, guarded by Nose Ring and Pink Pajamas. About two dozen kids pack into too small a space. They range from teens to toddlers lounging on tiny beanbag chairs or sprawled on the low-pile carpet. A few of the smaller ones horse around on a mat of spongy jigsaw pieces. In the corner, other kids play with a short, hand-cranked conveyor belt moving small cardboard boxes, pretending to be warehouse workers.

The commotion drops to a still silence; all eyes focus on me and my friends.

"Is this a daycare center?" I ask Anarchy Now.

"Preschool. We've fortified it as much as we can, and everyone who's toilet trained has a job. We've got scouts, watch duty, scavenging teams for food and supplies, a strategy and tactics committee, minders for the little ones, which is the hardest job of all . . . Anyway, welcome to the Feral Gang."

I take my first relaxed breath since I woke up this morning. The Feral Gang is organized. Tank and Gloriana and I don't have to make every decision by ourselves now. We aren't alone.

"I am so happy you're in charge," I tell Anarchy Now.

"She's not in charge. I am." A little girl steps forward out of the crowd. She resembles a dandelion with an untidy wisp of blond hair. She's young enough that the tooth fairy is probably a good source of personal income. Also, she needs to wipe her nose.

"What are you, seven?" blurts Gloriana.

"I'm nine," she shoots back. "How are old are *you*?"

"Twelve. Which means I'm one of you plus a toddler."

"Despite your weird toddler math, I don't see any advantage to age in a world where adults are trying to devour us."

"Fair," concedes Gloriana with reluctance. "But I find your mature vocabulary disquieting."

"My name's Bobbie Feral, and this is my Feral Gang. When was the last time you ate?"

Tank's stomach rumbles. "It's been a while."

Bobbie Feral turns to Anarchy Now. "Gladys, can you get them some nutrition?"

"I'm on it, boss."

A couple of minutes later, Anarchy Now brings out paper plates of Goldfish crackers, Cheerios, and juice boxes.

To me, it's a banquet. Bobbie looks on with satisfaction while my friends and I scarf it down. In a few minutes, my energy starts to return. And as my body recovers from all the stress, so does my sense of hope.

"Feeling better?" Bobbie asks.

"So much better. Thank you for the food and for taking us in."

"You're welcome. Kids need to band together during a crisis."

I heartily agree. "Anarchy Now . . . Gladys . . . said you have a plan for dealing with the consumers—that's what we've been calling the zombies. How can we help?"

"Keegan's got a plan, too," Tank says proudly.

Bobbie raises her eyebrows. "Oh, does he? I'd love to hear it."

"It's not really much of a plan. I'm sure yours is better."

"Yours is great," Tank encourages. "Go on, Keegan, tell them. Tell them your great plan."

Bashful, I tell the Feral Gang how the combination of implants and advertising created the consumers, and about Tank's tripwire, and the shock-delivering Automals.

"Interesting," says Bobbie. "How are you going to change the advertising to make 'consumers' want to play with Automals?"

"That part's a bit fuzzy," I confess. "But now that we're here, maybe we can put our heads together and figure it out. Any ideas?"

By now most of the Feral Gang has gathered close. They all look at each other, mostly silent. There are a few head shakes and shoulder shrugs.

"Nope," Bobbie concludes. "So, we're gonna go with my idea. Maxwell, bring over my plan."

Pink Pajamas wheels over a shopping cart piled with

staplers and tape dispensers and paperweights and big wooden building blocks.

"Ta-da," Bobbie says.

"Um, this is the plan?"

"Yeah. We're going to throw things at the zombies."

"But won't that hurt them?"

"If we're lucky."

Gloriana's eyes go wide, as if she's beholding a beautiful vision. "I love this plan!"

That's not necessarily a good thing. "I have a couple more questions, if that's okay?"

Bobbie doesn't seem bothered. "Let's hear them."

"That's a lot of ammunition, but there're thousands of consumers. How are you going to get them all?"

"We do it neighborhood by neighborhood. Our scouting reports indicate that in the adjacent three blocks, there are only . . . how many zombies, Gladys?"

"Fourteen."

"We can handle fourteen. Once they're dealt with, we retrieve our ammunition and move on to the next neighborhood."

I hate the idea of anyone hurling a stapler at my mom. I don't want to hurt *anyone*. But my plan isn't pain-free either.

Tank frowns. "This scheme only works if the consumers

are clustered together. How are you going to manage that?"

"I've given this a lot of consideration," Bobbie says. "We have to bait them."

"What's the bait?" asks Gloriana. "You have a stash of Meat Cramwiches?"

"No, we figured we'd tie one of us to a light post outside. Fresh meat should draw them like flies to a spilled ice cream cone."

"That's called a 'tethered goat,'" Tank says. "I learned that from a book, *Ropes and Roses*. She's a rodeo star, he's a florist, and . . . that's not important right now."

Gloriana's eyes narrow. "Who's the goat?"

"That's the one flaw in our plan," says. "Nobody's volunteered." She gives Tank a hard look. "Until now."

She snaps her fingers.

The Feral Gang forms a circle around us.

"Get the rope," she says.

EIGHTEEN

Tank strains against the ropes binding him to the lamppost. "I think we need to talk about what 'volunteer' means."

It had taken a lot of work to wrestle him down to the carpet, tie him up, and drag him outside. Many of the Ferals have bloody noses and blooming bruises. But in the end, even my mighty friend couldn't overcome their numbers.

He had not battled alone. Gloriana resisted like a rabid wolverine, and she didn't care whom she hit, kicked, elbow smashed, clotheslined, pile-drived, scratched, head-butted, body-avalanched, stinger-struck, chop-dropped, or bit to protect Tank.

I fought, too.

I think I earned an A for effort and a D-minus for effectiveness.

Gloriana and I are on the sidewalk, each with our own brutish teenager to restrain us in wrestling holds. A third hulking teen stands ready with a heavy building block to clobber us if we make too much trouble.

"Let him go!" I holler for the hundredth time. My throat feels like raw hamburger.

Gloriana snarls and growls.

Bobbie Feral holds a snow globe paperweight. It contains a model of Happy Town in sparkly water. "Calm down," she says. "Just because your friend's bait don't mean he's gonna get ate. Pretty soon we're gonna have zombies clustering around him and then we're gonna throw stuff with all our hearts. As soon as the zombies are all too dizzy or headachy or whatever to be a threat, we'll pull up stakes and repeat the maneuver somewhere else. And we'll keep doing it as many times as we have to until the zombies learn to stop craving our flesh."

"If it's so safe, why don't you be the bait?" I snap.

"Because there's vision, and then there's the labor it takes to make vision a reality. I'm a vision person." She glances down the street. "Oh, hey, looks like we got our first fish."

A bleary-eyed consumer stumbles around the corner. When he spots Tank he breaks into a floppy-gaited run.

Bobbie rolls her shoulders and tightens her grip on the

snow globe. "I promise, your buddy's going to be fine." She heads off to join the rest of the gang.

"He better be!" I call after her.

As it turns out, Bobbie is right. The lone consumer gets within ten feet of Tank before the Ferals pelt him with projectiles. One kid's stapler scores a direct hit on the temple.

"Owww!" the consumer whines, rubbing his sore head. "Why're you kids so awful? I just want to eat your large friend."

Bobbie answers by launching her snow globe. It shatters against the consumer's forehead, glass and sparkly water spilling to the street. The consumer wails, turns tail, and runs away.

The Ferals cheer as if they've won a war.

Another two consumers come around the corner.

"I did my part," Tank says to Bobbie. "Can it be someone else's turn now?"

"Ready the missiles," Bobbie calls in response.

Four more consumers join the other two.

"Aim!"

Yet more consumers turn the corner, and a white noise rises in the still air. Murmurs. Mumbling. Feet dragging against the pavement.

"That sounds like *a lot* of consumers," Gloriana says.

A whole crowd forms, dozens of ragged Happy Town adults, exhausted, nothing but vicious hunger in their eyes. They approach slowly but inevitably, like a toothy crocodile when you're mired in quicksand.

"There's too many of them," I warn Bobbie. "Let Tank go! You can't fight them all!"

To my surprise and relief, Bobbie Feral looks sensibly frightened. "I think . . . I think he's right. Maxwell, untie him."

Pink Pajamas rushes up to the light pole and struggles with the knot.

"Could you hurry, please?" Tank asks, his eyes widening as more consumers approach.

Pink Pajamas works at the rope, flustered. "Don't rush me. I don't do good work when people rush me."

There's one quiet instant when time seems to pause. It's the instant before a dam breaks and lets loose a flood. The space between falling off your skateboard and hitting the asphalt. Just enough time to know something horrible is about to happen.

The moment ends.

The consumer mob charges like a storm, a liquid mass, roiling and swirling, riding on a wave of bestial grunts and babbling.

Dozens of them?

Hundreds?

The Ferals launch their missiles. Several consumers go down, but for every consumer hit, three more replace them. I stop perceiving them as human. They're a force of nature. An avalanche. A disaster.

To his credit, Pink Pajamas doesn't abandon Tank. But neither does he manage to loosen the knot.

"Stand your ground and reload," Bobbie Feral screams. "Fire when you see the whites of their eyes. Which is right now. And bloodshot eyes count as white."

Feral hands reach into the cart, taking up every available projectile. They chuck their missiles at the advancing wave. Consumers spill to the pavement, clutching their heads or noses or knees, wherever they're struck. But there are so many of them.

With a fearsome war cry, Bobbie Feral plows the now-empty cart into the front wave of consumers, dropping them like bowling pins. But what counts as a strike when there are so many more pins?

The teens guarding Gloriana and me loosen their grips and scramble to help their fellow Ferals.

I know what I have to do.

"Gloriana, untie Tank. I'll deal with the consumers."

"How?"

My fingers dip into my pocket for the only useful resource in my possession: the stale Happy Chicken Nugget. I didn't know exactly what I was going to do with it when I found it at the puppet theater, but I thought it might come in handy if I ended up having to bargain with a consumer for my life. Now, I'm going to use it to put my life at more risk.

Stepping into the street, I thrust it high over my head like a sword.

"BEHOLD!" I roar. "NUGGET MEAT!"

The consumers slow, skidding and stumbling.

Their horrific noise drops down to a muttering hum.

Hundreds of eyes focus on the nugget as if drawn to a magnet.

"Keegan, no," whispers Gloriana.

I wink at her. I don't know precisely what the wink means, but I figure it's the sort of thing a cool heroic person would do.

"Bite me!" I shout at the mob.

Then I run away.

NINETEEN

I've been scared before.

I was scared the first time I rode a bike after my dad told me that I was certainly going to fall. It turned out he was right, but he didn't warn me that the pedal would cut up my shin, and then I was even more scared getting back on the bike because I knew I was going to fall again.

I was scared when Mom and Dad got into a fight over it.

I was scared when they got divorced, and scared when Mom started dating Carl, because I knew my life was going to keep changing, and some of those changes would be good, but some of them wouldn't.

I was scared the first time I had a cavity drilled.

As I run from the consumers, this fear feels different.

There's no thinking involved. This is the ancient fear of a tiny mammal hunted by an allosaurus. This is the fear of monsters.

Every step I take draws the consumers farther away from my friends, so I keep running with the stale Happy Nugget held high. This is what heroes do. They run until something eats their legs.

I have the advantage of speed because I'm young and resilient. But the consumers have the advantage of being wracked with monstrous appetite. When one falls, there are others to continue the pursuit. If I fall, the consumers will be flossing Keegan morsels out of their teeth.

When I turn down an alley, I find a consumer gnawing on a leather shoe.

I swallow a startled scream and hold my breath.

The consumer's nostrils twitch, and she turns her head to me so fast her neck cracks. "Liver," she says, in such a matter-of-fact tone that I feel spiders skitter across my belly.

Turning tail, I beg my legs for one more burst of speed.

Back on the main avenue, another contingent of consumers pick over the scant remains of a trash bin. I cast around for anything to conceal myself behind: a tree, a bush, a fire hydrant. But the sterile streets of Happy Town provide nothing.

The consumers lift their noses to the air and abandon the bin. Like a wolf pack, they separate and spread out, spanning the width of the street from sidewalk to sidewalk.

I can almost feel their fingertips brushing the back of my neck.

I can almost feel their hot breath.

I can almost feel their incisors piercing my flesh.

Part of me wants to lie down on the pavement and wait for them to spring. I'm so tired. Not just from physical exertion, not the moment-by-moment struggle to stay alive, but from the constant terror. Part of me wants to give in to the inevitable and get it over with.

But a bigger part tells the small part to shut up. The bigger part still cares about my mom, about Tank and Gloriana. The bigger part still wants to survive.

The consumer pack tightens their circle. They'll attack any second now.

"Hey look," says a voice from the crowd, "that kid's arm comes with a free nugget!"

It is time for me and my nugget friend to go our separate ways.

"Happy Nugget," I tell my nugget, "your hero moment has arrived."

I launch it as far as I can, not even choosing a direction, just sending it in a high arc. The breading glistens like a rainbow.

Making guttural noises that might have included the words "flying" and "chicken," the pack breaks off to chase it down.

All but one.

This one wears a harsh yellow vest with reflective stripes over mechanic's coveralls. His knuckles are swollen, fingernails bloody. He stumbles with a limp, eyes cast down at his own ankle as if to make sure it's still working.

"Don't bother hunting me," I say, trying to sound brave. "I can outrun you."

"Can you?" His voice his rough, probably overstrained by calling for meat. But something about it is familiar.

Carl. My stepfather.

Dark circles ring his eyes. Bloods seeps from a cut down his cheek. He licks his bleeding lips.

"Listen, Keegan. Don't run. Just listen." Carl takes a step toward me.

"No. I've already been through this with Mom."

"You saw your mom? Is she okay?"

"NOBODY IS OKAY, CARL!"

"I just want to help you, Keegan." Another step.

"You're not my real dad."

"I know. But I am an elevator mechanic, and I know how you can get somewhere safe."

"Stop limping at me." I move to keep distance. "You just want to eat me."

"And if I hadn't sprained my ankle, I'd be doing it already. So shut up and listen to me. Go three blocks up. Then left. Then two more blocks. There's a phone booth. Pick up the receiver. Press the numbers to spell out 'galaxy brain.'"

"Is this a trick?"

"Do I look sharp enough to play tricks right now? I said I'm an elevator mechanic. The phone booth is an elevator."

"This seems pretty far-fetched, Carl."

"Even with this ankle I can still make a lunge. I might get you." He licks his lips again.

I stand frozen with indecision. Can I trust Carl?

And can I leave him alone in the street with an injury?

A tear streams down his face. "Please just go before I tear your arm off like a drumstick."

"Carl, I . . ."

"*Please*, Keegan."

"Okay. I just want to say sorry about the 'real dad' crack. You annoy me but you're okay. You make Mom happy and you've always been pretty good to me, and even my real dad thinks you're okay, and—"

"GO!" Carl roars.

This time, I do.

Only too late does a question occur to me: What's a phone booth?

TWENTY

Following my carnivorous zombie stepdad's directions, I find a glass coffin on a street corner. It stands vertically against yet another white, gray, and pale-green building. Inside is a toolbox-sized telephone device. This must be a phone booth. Or else it's an old-time World War II radio.

I don't have a lot of time to figure it out, because the intersection starts filling with consumers.

I give the booth's door a yank and it unfolds like an accordion bellows. Let's see if I can get this phone device to work. Carl said to pick up the receiver. By that he must have meant the plastic horn-like thing hanging from a hook. Both ends of the horn are shaped like mini-muffins with holes in them. I lift it from the hook and put it up to my ear. It buzzes.

"Hello? This is Keegan, come in please, over." The hum continues. "Happy Town is having a dire emergency and we need help, over. Does anybody read, over?"

Nothing.

Dizzy with fatigue, I lean my back against the side of the phone booth and try to remember what else Carl told me to do.

Punch a galaxy brain? I would love to as long as the galaxy brain is Arlo Corn.

But Carl must have meant the buttons with letters and numbers printed on them.

While slack-jawed consumers limp and lurch in my direction, I punch in "G-A-L-A-X-Y-B-R-A-I . . ."

Too late.

A consumer with blood in his teeth scratches the glass door. He's soon joined by his fellow cannibals. They swarm over the phone booth like ants on an apple pie.

One of them finds the door handle and yanks.

I grab it from the inside and yank back.

I am now engaged in a life-or-death yank battle with a zombie.

He's winning.

He's going to eat me.

I'm going to die.

And what will be the last thing I see?

It won't be the ocean. Or a field of wildflowers. Or a tree.

It won't be my mom's face.

It won't be Tank or Gloriana, who've become important to me in a very short time, because one of them has a big open heart and declared me a best friend within two seconds of meeting me and the other doesn't go with the flow, doesn't care about the flow, is actually very anti-flow, and I have come to realize that sometimes the flow is utter horse poo.

No. The last thing I see will be gnashing teeth.

Unless I fight harder.

With one hand on the door handle, the other straining to reach the buttons, my survival is now a matter of millimeters.

But it's not just my survival. I don't even know where my friends are right now, assuming they're still alive. If I don't get to the Fulfillment Center and somehow release the Automals to electrically shock every adult in Happy Town, the day will end with blood and gristle and death.

So I pull harder to keep the phone booth door shut, and

I reach farther, farther, farther, straining my shoulder ligaments until my fingernail touches the last button: N.

The phone booth pivots. With a grinding, grating noise, bricks in the side of the building separate, exposing a hidden portal. The phone booth slides on rails into the building, and the bricks slide back shut in the faces of frustrated consumers. The booth shoots up an elevator shaft, and my heart soars with relief.

Maybe this is an escape pod! Maybe it'll launch me out of Earth's atmosphere, freeing me from the bonds of gravity and the headaches of consumers. But what would I do in space? Would I get picked up by a shuttle? Would I dock with a space station? Would I fly beyond Earth's orbit to the moon or Mars or deep space? And do I trust Arlo Corn to build his own space program? Considering the way things are going in Happy Town, absolutely not.

Fortunately, the phone booth does not turn out to be a space-faring escape craft. Instead it comes to a stop at a high floor. A pair of exterior doors parts to reveal an unexpected sight: beauty.

I step out of the phone booth into a covered walkway. This must be one of the elevated sidewalks that connects the higher floors of the tallest buildings. There are probably access points like the phone booth all over the city so Corn can move around Happy Town without being bothered by employees. He could probably get anywhere he wanted from here: to his office, or to visit his bottled severed heads, or to the Fulfillment Center.

My sneakers touch soft grass. Vines with vivid purple and blue flowers trail from the ceiling. Ferns and exotic tropical plants border the path. The air smells like nothing else in Happy Town—sweet, clean, and natural. When a butterfly flits by my nose, broad orange wings and deep black ink lines, I wonder if maybe I died some time ago and this is heaven. Then I spot a bronze plaque embedded in the grass like a grave marker: It says "Private Sidewalk Reserved for Arlo Corn."

Creeping down the path, listening for any sign of consumers, all I hear is the ripple of water. I come upon a koi pond where plump orange and white and black and speckled fish the size of foot-long submarine sandwiches cruise below the surface of clear water.

There are no consumers up here. Fish is meat, and consumers would have left behind nothing but skeletons and scattered fish scales.

I could lie in the grass, listen to the gentle gurgles of

the pond, rest my exhausted muscles and heart and lungs. But every second I waste increases the chances of Tank and Gloriana and the Ferals and all the other plucky youth being eaten.

With a groan, I break into a run and follow the path.

TWENTY-ONE

The lights flicker, alternating between utter darkness and lightning-bright flashes. Between the flashes I look down from the elevated walkway upon a writhing mass of consumers. They roam between the high Fulfillment Center shelves like the probing tendrils of a giant living organism.

The whole place is trashed—mountains of toppled boxes, their lids clawed open and contents spilled everywhere. Anything that contained meat must be long gone.

Searching for a way to the Fulfillment Center floor, I find an escalator marked with a brass plaque that says "Private Escalator Reserved for Arlo Corn."

The lights go off. This is my chance. I race down the escalator to the dark warehouse floor. Odors strike me like a punch in the nose when I reach the bottom: sweet, floral, and musky all at once. My eyes water, and it takes a mighty act of will to keep from sneezing. It's Sniffree. A very strong, concentrated version of it.

Low moans and whimpers from desperate consumers surround me. Once the lights come back on, they'll strip me to the bone like museum beetles.

I take a step in the direction of the Automal cage, and something crunches under my foot. It's just a small sound, but it might as well be a bomb going off. The consumers' utterings fall silent. I freeze, not daring to take another step. My nostrils fill with the stinging scent of Sniffree.

"Don't you dare, nostrils," I telepathically warn my nostrils. "Don't you dare sneeze."

"Sorry," my nostrils say back. "We are totally going to sneeze."

"If you sneeze, we're dead."

"We'd rather die than live with Sniffree inside us."

"Cowards!"

Perhaps shamed by my accusation, my nostrils hold the sneeze in long enough for the consumers to go back to shuffling and muttering.

I tiptoe in the general direction of the Automal cage.

Probing the darkness with my hands in front of me, I hope I don't end up inserting my fingers right into the mouth of a slavering consumer.

I tell myself that this is not a pitch-dark warehouse full of cannibals. This is just a haunted house at the county fair. The consumers are just actors hired to give me an entertaining fright. Once I'm out of the dark I'll visit the livestock exhibits. I'll check out the blue-ribbon pie winners. I'll get some kettle corn. Maybe a churro.

I do not find a churro, but my hip contacts something metallic. It's chain link. I made it!

And just as I'm experiencing this joyous thought, the lights flicker on. Consumers gape at me. They blink in wondrous confusion, as if racks of spareribs have fallen from the sky.

"Thank you for showing up," one of them says. "We really appreciate it."

"Buuuuuuh," says another in rougher shape.

I force on a cheerful smile. "If you could just not tear my flesh with your teeth for a few minutes, I can fix your hunger. You'll be yourselves again instead of gripped by an insatiable desire for my kidneys."

"Oooh, kidneys," says one.

"I love kidneys," says another.

"All the guts are tasty," says a third.

"I am so tired of adults wanting my giblets" say I.

I race into the cage and clang the gate shut behind me. Poking my fingers through the mesh, I slide the deadbolt into place. It won't last, but it might give me the few minutes I need.

The recharged Automals are strewn about the floor. Some have tooth marks. I imagine consumers had hoped for raw animal meat and been disappointed by fake fur and plastic. If the Automals had been powered on, they would have tasted a jolt of electricity.

I grab a piglet at random. Green pinpoints glow in the center of its black-glass eyes, indicating a full battery charge.

A cluster of consumers form around the cage. They tug at the cage door, fumble with the deadbolt, rattle the mesh, call me dirty names like "kidney sausage."

Ignoring them, I turn the piglet belly-up to expose the tiny power button. With a press the little pig squeals, its coiled tail wiggling with programmed excitement. Then, *ZZZZZZZZTTT.* The piglet discharges electricity into my fingers. I bite my lip against the mix of ache and burn and numbness traveling up my arm.

Getting shocked is a good thing. It means my plan has a hope of working. I set the pig's course for maximum scamper, endure another eye-watering shock, and set it on the ground. The pig scurries away to do my bidding.

Next I snap up a skunk and power it on. *ZZZZzzzt!* Wincing in pain, I command myself not to drop it; then I open the gate and chuck it at the nearest consumer.

ZZZZzzzt! "OUCH!"

Now, a squirrel. It gives me another shock, but I don't slow down, because heroes don't quit, even when being electrocuted by adorable malfunctioning animals.

I suffer an elephant.

I blink tears and release a guinea-pig-sized cow.

I yelp and let loose a guinea-pig-sized guinea pig.

I get into a rhythm: One, snatch animal. Two, turn it on. Three, hiss in pain. Four, release animal. Cuss and repeat.

"Be free and shock grown-ups," I exhort my pain-delivering menagerie.

Will this work? I'm about to find out. A consumer stumbles toward me. She displays the now-familiar bruises and abrasions the consumers inflict on one another.

"Is that meat?" she croaks.

"One, don't call me a 'that.' I'm a person. Two, I'm not meat. Three, look at all those cute little scuttling meat animals all around you. Don't they look scrumptious?"

"Enh, those are toys, not meat. You're meat."

"No, listen, I'm telling you, the little animals are meat. You just let a tiny hippo zip right past you."

Another consumer approaches. "Did I hear meat?" This one steps over a speeding robot tortoise.

The babble of consumers grows more organized, a single word rising above the rest, repeated until it becomes a synchronized chant by hundreds of voices: "Meat! Meat! Meat! Meat!"

My vision tunnels. My world is reduced to dismal sensations. The meat chant. My heartbeat pounding in my head. The stench of Sniffree. The sights of bloody faces, red-rimmed eyes, parched lips, pasty gums, and gnashing teeth.

One consumer picks up a speeding giraffe on reflex.

It's Ed Brown, Assistant Manager of Cardboard.

ZZzzzap!

"Ow!" He drops the giraffe and sucks on his fingers. "Where are your parents? I'm going to send them a sharply worded message."

"Right now my parents are trying to snack on my class-mates. Do you still want to eat my guts?"

Ed makes a sick face and puts a hand on his belly. "The very thought fills me with loathing and revulsion."

"Does that mean no?"

"Yes, it means no. I think I just had three pounds of raw ground beef. Or maybe it was a foot."

"I need your help, Ed Brown."

"You want my help? After you shocked me?"

"Can you stop thinking about yourself for a minute? Think of the children."

"Fine, what do you want?"

"Start picking up those Automals and pass them, throw them, do whatever it takes to shock the consumers."

"What's a consumer?"

"It's what you were. Like a brain-eating zombie, only less finicky."

"All right." Grudgingly, Ed Brown reaches down and grabs a fuzzy porcupine off the floor.

Zap! Zzzip! Zzzap!

"Oooowww!"

He flings the offending porcupine on reflex and the Automal strikes another consumer in the face.

"OOOWWW WHAT THE HECK, ED?!?"

Nobody in this scene is having a good time. But I keep tossing activated Automals out of the cage, and a few cured consumers catch on and actually start helping. And like a chain reaction, the more people who help, the more consumers are cured.

While adults continue to switch on and release Automals, I leave the cage, hook my fingers through the mesh, and climb. From this high vantage, I can see beyond the cured consumers to the hundreds still rampaging and hungry for meat. The process is going too slow.

"Those of you who are cured, you have a job to do," I call out, summoning my loudest voice. I blink in surprise when I realize I've just started delivering a stirring speech. I wish Tank were here. But he's not. It's up to me. "You're not working for Happy Town now. And not for Arlo Corn either. You're working for everyone who's been used and hurt by his greed. Shock the zombie next to you! Shock your coworkers! Shock your neighbors! Shock your friends and husbands and wives! If they're an adult, shock them! Wake them up!"

Nobody cheers.

Nobody pledges to follow my leadership.

Nobody declares me a hero.

But the electrical snaps and pops and sharp exclamations of pain sound better than any of that. Adults are doing what I tell them to do.

Still, the Fulfillment Center is a massive, sprawling place, and there remain thousands of consumers all over Happy Town and hundreds of kids in danger.

I climb down and return to the cage. "There're too many zombies to hand Automals off one by one," I tell Ed Brown. "We need to make people want them and seek them out. Does anyone know where the ad boards and blimps are controlled from?"

"I do," says a grim-faced woman with a strong jaw and steel in her eyes. She looks like a coach or a drill sergeant or someone else who tells you to do push-ups and you do even though your arms feel like rubber bands but you'd rather suffer push-ups than suffer her wrath.

"Gather round, maggots!" she barks. She organizes a crew of bodyguards who form a protective circle around me. With them as my shield, we set off to another part of the Fulfillment Center.

Progress is a battle of inches, tiny step after tiny step as more consumers accumulate in my orbit. My escorts scuffle with consumers trying to grab at me and tear me apart like tufts of cotton candy.

"Hold the line!" orders Push-up Woman. "Don't let them through!"

My guards put up a valiant effort, shoving consumers back and batting away grasping hands. I feel the heat from the press of consumer bodies. Sweat streams down my forehead like tears. The moans and cries and demands for meat combine in a jet-engine roar.

When I started converting consumers with the Automals, I allowed myself a spark of hope, but that was a mistake. I'm the prize tuna in a shark feeding frenzy, and this time there's no way out of it.

"Don't worry," Push-up Woman shouts in my ear. "If they break through and eat you, it'll be over quick."

One of the guards panics and abandons my wall of protection. Before the remaining bodyguards can close the gap, a consumer's arm reaches through them and grabs a fistful of my hair. I thrash to release the grip, screaming with pain as hair tears loose from my scalp.

People say in your final moments, your life flashes before your eyes. You replay your fondest and saddest moments, your greatest triumphs and most heartbreaking tragedies. You think of your friends, your families, your loved ones. You think of times when you were at peace, and times when you suffered terrors.

You think of a miniature kangaroo sailing over your head. Followed by a tortoise. And a polar bear. And a chimpanzee.

Wait.

The Automals aren't a vision. They're real, and they're just the first raindrops of a storm. The air fills with barrages of hurled Automals, an entire zoo of them, well aimed to soar over my head and land in the thick consumer mob.

Yelps of pain spurt from the din. Zapped consumers fling the Automals away, only for them to be caught by other consumers. Animals pop out of the crowd like corn kernels, and within moments, the mob's violent energy begins to drain away. For every ravenous consumer, there's a cured grown-up.

Through the thinned consumer glut, my eyes land a glorious sight.

It is a hero. I can tell by his pose. In his right hand, he grips a platypus. In his left, a manatee.

"Tank! My large and high-spirited friend!"

He lobs his Automals.

"Eat voltage," shouts a voice. It's Gloriana, launching a narwhal.

"Gloriana! My violent friend!"

A tidal wave of relief washes over me. They're still alive! They made it! And they're here, right now, with me, giving us a fighting chance.

Also, they didn't come alone. They brought the Feral Gang—Pink Pajamas, Nose Ring, Anarchy Now, and Bobbie Feral with all the little kids, along with carts piled with Automals, which they launch in salvo after salvo at the remaining consumers.

Gloriana hurls a wolverine and barks, "Reload!" She holds out an impatient hand until Bobbie Feral places an ocelot in it. Gloriana lets it fly. She holds out her hand again. "You're slowing down, Bobbie. Reload!"

Bobbie Feral supplies her with a ring-tailed lemur.

"You heard the boss," says Tank. "Keep up the pace and we can win this battle."

"Gloriana's in charge of the Feral Gang now?" I manage to sputter.

"It's the Gloriana Gang now," Gloriana says. "Tank gave a stirring speech and convinced everyone that I'm the best qualified to lead a gang of object-tossing youths."

"We are witnessing Gloriana in the midst of her hero moment," Tank enthuses.

Gloriana hurls a dromedary camel. "Give me another or I'll knock your block off, Bobbie Feral!"

"And you helped her achieve it, Tank! That means you had your own hero moment."

"That's right! And now I can devote myself one hundred percent to being a helpful side character."

"You kids inspire me," Push-up Woman says. "But we don't have time for inspiration. We're at the server room." My bodyguards have delivered me to a plain white door. "Now get in there and do whatever you're gonna do. C'mere, Marvin." A rather banged-up man with lank hair staggers over. "Marvin's a computer whiz, so he's going in with you."

After so many adults have tried to eat me or abandoned me and my friends via helicopter, I find myself choked with emotion. "Thank you for choosing to help us, ma'am."

She grunts and hurls a wallaby.

"I'm coming with you, Keegan," says Tank.

"Me too," Gloriana asserts. "Bobbie, you're in charge. Don't screw this up or —"

"You'll knock my block off, I know. When this is over,

Gloriana, you and me are going to see who's the better block knocker."

Bobbie Feral chucks a sugar glider, and my friends and I dart inside the server room to enter the final phase of Arlo Corn's disaster.

TWENTY-TWO

Finally, something in Happy Town doesn't disappoint. The server room resembles NASA mission control with tiered rows of computer workstations and a wall-sized monitor screen ringed by smaller screens. The only letdown is that instead of tracking a spaceship to Mars, the large screen plays the Meat Cramwich ad. The smaller screens display environmental factors inside the dome—oxygen levels, carbon dioxide, temperature, humidity, atmospheric pressure. Other screens show live surveillance footage from outside the Fulfillment Center, and every view offers a different horror. Consumer mobs flood streets. Kids dive into trash dumpsters or scramble up undersized trees to escape. The crisis isn't over.

I throw myself into a chair at one of the workstations. With a few clicks of the mouse, a screen pops up with the words "Systems Master Control" along with a log-in box.

"Marvin, what's the password?"

Marvin shrugs. "I don't know."

"But the scary push-up person said you're a computer whiz."

"I am, but that doesn't mean I have all the passwords."

Gloriana looks around for anything to toss. "Can't you hack into the system?"

"I can hack into anything. As long as I have the password."

I bury my face in my hands. "I cannot believe this. Could we have an adult who can take care of things for five seconds? We're *so* close to winning."

"We have to hang in there," Tank says. "Remember what I said about the Extreme Leader and his Shadow Empire?"

"After every win there's another inevitable failure?"

"I don't think that's quite what I said."

I put my fingers on the keyboard.

"Try 'PASSWORD,'" Marvin suggests. "That's the default, and a lot of people never bother changing it."

"This is not going to work," I mutter as I type "PASS-WORD."

And I am right. The words "Failed log-in attempt" display on the screen, followed by "You have two more attempts."

I draw a breath and type "GALAXYBRAIN."

The same message appears, only now it says "You have one more attempt."

"Try 'Don't trust Corn,'" Gloriana offers.

"Just make sure it's at least twelve characters long and has a capital letter and a lowercase letter and a number and a special character," says Marvin.

"Now you tell me?"

On the screen, the tree-climber runs out of branches while consumers gather around the trunk.

"C'mon, think," I whisper to myself. "Think about everything you've been through this week. Think about what you've learned about Happy Town. Think about what you've learned about the world and people and how things really work. The challenges and obstacles you've overcome are the key to achieving your hero moment. You've got one chance. What's the password?"

I type.

The log-in screen goes away, replaced by a program interface.

"I'm in!"

"YES!" cheers Tank. "I knew you could do it, and I'm so happy to be here to share this moment with you! What was the password?"

"Meatcramwichthemicrowaveablemeatsandwichcram medwithmeat with a 'one' and an exclamation point."

"You are brilliant," Tank concludes.

Navigating menus, I find a New Ad option. It brings up a text window.

"What should I type?"

"Effective advertising appeals to emotional needs and desires," Tank says.

I draw a long breath and return my hands to the keyboard. "Automals, the perfect companions. Love them. Crave them. Do whatever you must to snatch one. Get emotional fulfillment now at the Fulfillment Center."

"Not exactly poetry," says Marvin.

Gloriana's search for something to throw grows more urgent.

"Where would you like to display new ad?" reads the screen.

I click every option available: Billboards. Blimps. TVs. Refrigerator screens. Happy Town streaming services. Loudspeakers.

The computer goes "bing."

A few seconds of corny music plays.

A whole menagerie of Automals appear on the screen.

Then a voice: "Automals! The perfect companions! Love them! Crave them . . ."

The entire ad plays. Then again. Over and over.

The consumer cacophony outside the door doesn't die, but it changes.

"Automals!" someone screams.

"I love them," rasps someone else.

"I crave them!"

"GIVE ME AN AUTOMAL! I WANT AN AUTO-MAL!"

"I WOULD PREFER A ROBOT PUPPY BUT I WILL TAKE A ROBOT ANYTHING!"

"AUTOMALS! AUTOMALS! AUTOMALS!"

I dare crack the door open. A consumer stampede rushes past, ignoring me. No hands come for me. No one gnashes their teeth.

The consumers no longer want meat.

They only want fuzzy toy animals that deliver electrical shocks.

I monitor the consumers of Happy Town over the surveillance screens. The pack trying to get at the kid up the tree disperses. Consumers leave a kid hiding in the garbage bin alone. Zombie nests emerge from the hospital and other buildings and parade toward the Fulfillment Center.

Tank gives me a congratulatory slap on the shoulder. "You did it, Keegan!"

"Not yet. If those consumers get here and there aren't enough Automals to greet them with a zap, we might have a riot on our hands."

I'll have to organize some kind of bucket brigade with employees activating more Automals and others carting them to the Fulfillment Center entrance. Once the consumers flooding to the Fulfillment Center are cured, I'll get to work assigning the Automals to outlying parts of town by the MICE network. If they're set to maximum scurry, they'll eventually end up in the hands of every consumer. It'll take thousands of zaps, but in a few hours, this nightmare could be over.

When I exit the server room with Tank and Gloriana,

I'm shocked to find adults already doing all the things I thought of. They're banding together, pitching in, working to fix things.

They're helping.

Over the next couple of hours, I do the unthinkable. I trust the adults of Happy Town.

It's a time for reunions.

It's a time for apologies.

It's a time for bandages.

Adults set themselves to work with brooms and forklifts and tools to clean and repair things in the Fulfillment Center and beyond. Others form a makeshift infirmary to help the injured. Search parties set out to find kids who are still hiding and anyone who's too hurt to get to the Fulfillment Center. They bring Automals with them, just in case.

Parents and kids and coworkers and neighbors and friends find each other. There are hugs and tears.

Gloriana and Bobbie Feral even shake hands.

"Keegan! Oh, my boy!" Mom comes rushing from the crowd and engulfs me in an embrace. "I am so sorry," she sobs. "I promise to never, ever, ever again let anybody connect an implant to my brain that makes me want to rip your limbs off and turn them on a rotisserie for seventy minutes with garlic and rosemary and white pepper served with a fresh green salad."

"That was very specific, Mom."

"You know I love to cook."

"I was just going to eat him raw." It's Carl.

"That is gross," I inform him.

"I thought you liked sushi."

"I'm not fish, Carl."

"No. No, you're not. You're okay."

It not a question. It's a statement.

"Yeah. You're okay, too."

We shake on being okay.

"You guys should get checked out at the infirmary," I tell Mom and Carl. "I'm gonna go back to my friends. We'll catch up later."

Mom and Carl agree that we will.

I find Tank and Gloriana reuniting with their own parents and sending them off to get their cuts and abrasions taken care of.

The world has taken a sharp turn for the better. But I can't shake the feeling that something isn't right. "My body feels weird. My legs won't stop twitching. My heart's still pounding. My brain is hot."

"Maybe you have an infection," Gloriana suggests. "Maybe you've contracted a tropical parasite."

Tank places a hand on my forehead to test my temperature. "We've been fighting for our lives, running on fear and adrenaline. It's going to take a while for our bodies to realize we don't have to fight anymore. But it'll pass."

And gradually, it does. Tank makes me sit on a box, and Gloriana goes in search of hydration and calories. She comes back with three Happy Town coffee mugs containing Slurries. Slowly slurping (mine tastes like red), my friends and I unclench and let the adults do the work. Maybe for the first time, Happy Town isn't just a company. Or even just a city. Maybe, strangely, through hardship, it's become a community.

My chest loosens. My heart no longer labors to pump blood to my muscles. My brain chills.

Things are quiet.

"Ten," a voice says over the loudspeakers. It's followed by a giggle.

"Nine. Eight."

"Yep," Tank says. "That's a countdown."

I shoot back to my feet. "What's it counting down?"

191

"Seven." Another giggle.

Gloriana releases her grip on her mug and lets it shatter on the floor. "Corn shredded papers and melted his computer to hide evidence. I bet he planted a bomb to make sure he didn't miss anything."

"Six."

I hate how much that makes sense.

The adults who'd been working together to convert chaos back into order choose chaos again. They abandon their tools and brooms. They run in no particular directions.

"Stop panicking," I holler. "If there's a bomb, we have to find it. We have to . . . I don't know . . . debomb the town!"

"Listen to us," pleads Gloriana. "We have experience with disasters!"

Nobody listens.

Half a dozen adults battle over possession of a football helmet, and I don't bother telling them that it's designed to prevent injury from tackles, not explosives.

"Four," says the voice. "Three."

I plug my ears and focus on my friends, hoping the sight of their faces washes away the vision flashing before my eyes: Carl and his stupid Sousaphone. Which is not the last thing I want to see before I die.

"Two. One."

Another giggle. Then, "Ignition."

Happy Town shakes as though a cosmic god has grabbed the dome with both hands to use as a colossal baby rattle. Light fixtures high overhead crash down. Boxes tumble from high shelves. A symphony of breaking glass. A chorus of thunder.

Other than the world breaking and everything falling apart, the only sounds are Arlo Corn's maddening giggle followed by two more words:

"Liftoff."

TWENTY-THREE

We stand on the edge of town, Tank and Gloriana and I, to stare out the dome.

Millions of stars shine across an impossibly black sky. They don't twinkle because there's no atmosphere in space to disturb their light.

We're supposed to be at a mandatory emergency meeting right now along with every other resident of Happy Town, but once we found out the main item on the agenda is figuring out how we're going to keep selling and shipping things from our current location, we decided to skip it. There'll probably be some kind of punishment, but the flow is stupid and we will not go with it.

Beneath my feet is . . . everything.

A skein of clouds. Here and there the spiraling vortex

of a tropical storm. Great patches of brown continents with fuzzy veils of green, all connected by the deep blue oceans from horizon to curved horizon.

"Changing your worldview is part of becoming a hero," Tank says. "And here we are, literally viewing the whole world."

"Mm-hmm," I respond.

"Look on the bright side," he says. "We're in space! How amazing is that? We thought we were living in a city, but turns out we've been on a giant spaceship all this time. I mean, sure, nobody asked if this is what we wanted. And our spaceship is trashed thanks to the whole consumer catastrophe. But, you know . . . space."

"Yep."

Gloriana points to the peak of the dome. "Is that a crack?"

I make out a thin white line in the glass. From here it looks like an eyelash, but it's got to be at least a yard long.

"Mm-hmm."

"And if it breaks all the way through the dome we'll lose our atmosphere and get sucked into the heartless cold vacuum of space," says Gloriana.

"I'm sure there're Happy Town employees with the tools and training to handle this sort of thing," Tank says.

"Mm-hmm."

I can only communicate in grunts and short syllables because I don't know what else to say.

What do you say when the world is awful only because a few people choose to make it that way?

What do you say when too many people are willing to go along with it?

What do you say when you've survived a zombie apocalypse only to wind up in a failing spaceship owned by the same dipstick who caused the zombie apocalypse?

As the crack grows from eyelash-length to head-hair length, a recording plays all over the city, from every screen, from every speaker, from every blimp. It's not encouraging.

Gloriana squares her shoulders and gazes up at the crack with a defiant tilt to her chin. "There's always another version of the Extreme Leader and his Shadow Empire, isn't that right, Tank?"

"It sure is, Gloriana. It sure is."

What do you say? What do you do?

I turn to my friends. "Let's find some glue."

TWENTY-FOUR

Please wait and remain happy. Help is on the way.

Please wait and remain happy. Help is on the way.

Please wait and remain happy. Help is on the way.

Please wait and remain happy. Help is on the way.

Please wait and remain happy. Help is on the way.

Please wait and remain happy. Help is on the way.

Please wait and remain happy. Help is on the way.

Please wait and remain happy. Help is on the way.

Please wait and remain happy. Help is on the way.

Please wait and remain happy. Help is on the way.

Please wait and remain happy. Help is on the way.

Please wait and remain happy. Help is on the way.

Please wait and remain happy. Help is on the way.

ACKNOWLEDGMENTS

I wrote this story by myself, but a massive labor force worked hard to turn it into a book and bring it to you. They include publishing workers, printers, warehouse workers, truck drivers and rail workers, wholesalers, booksellers, curriculum experts, librarians, teachers, and people in a whole lot of other occupations I'm not even aware of. I can't possibly thank them all by name, but I'm profoundly grateful to each and every one of them. They all deserve a good wage, good benefits, appreciation, and respect.

Happily, there are a bunch of hard-working people I *can* name. My agent Holly Root and her incredible team at Root Literary continually advance my cause and watch my back. At HarperCollins, Erica Sussman, my editor, invested a massive amount of time, thought, care, and energy to help me make my story the best it could be, as did the inestimable Clare Vaughn. My thanks go also to Jessica Berg, Abby Dommert, Michael Goldstein, Deanna Hoak, Robby Imfeld, Alison Klapthor, Chris Kwon, Emily Mannon, Gwen Morton, Vanessa Nuttry, and everybody in every department who had a hand in my book.

You can't buy friendship, which is good news for me, because I couldn't possibly pay my pals what they're worth for rendering advice, sympathy, commiseration, and encouragement, often without even knowing I needed it, or even that they provided it. Thank you, Rae Carson, Deb Coates, Charles Coleman Finlay, Oz Drummond, Karen Meisner, Sarah Prineas, and Jenn Reese.

Special shout to my dogs, Amelia and Dozer. They didn't help at all, but they amused me.

Finally, as always, my biggest thanks go to Lisa Will, who makes things possible and fun.

Thank you all so much for your work.